THE SWIVEL-EYED OGRE-THING

LOOK OUT FOR MORE
AMAZING
MONSTERS,
TOTAL HEROICS
AND A BIT OF
RUNNING AWAY IN

The Shark-Headed
Bear-Thing

The Moon-Faced
Ghoul-Thing

THE SWIVEL-EYED OGRE-Thing

BARRY HUTCHISON

illustrated by
CHRIS MOULD

nosy
crow

First published 2015 by Nosy Crow Ltd
The Crow's Nest, 10a Lant Street
London SE1 1QR
www.nosycrow.com

ISBN: 978 0 85763 306 4

Nosy Crow and associated logos are trademarks
and/or registered trademarks of Nosy Crow Ltd

Text © Barry Hutchison, 2015
Cover and inside illustrations © Chris Mould, 2015

The right of Barry Hutchison and Chris Mould to be identified as the author
and illustrator respectively has been asserted.

A CIP catalogue record for this book is available from the British Library.

Printed and bound in the UK by Clays Ltd, St Ives Plc.

Papers used by Nosy Crow are made from wood grown in
sustainable forests.

1 3 5 7 9 8 6 4 2

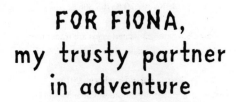

FOR FIONA,
my trusty partner
in adventure

B. H.

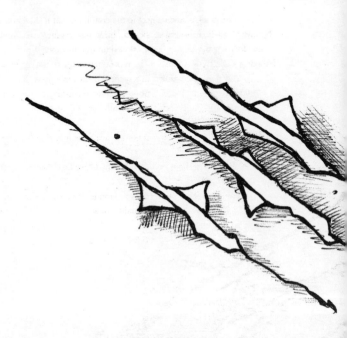

chapter One

Benjamin Blank had just scoffed down a Lump Hog sandwich for supper and was halfway up the stairs to bed when the screaming started. It shrieked from somewhere just outside the house, shaking the shuttered windows and squealing in through the gaps in the old stone walls.

Ben spun on the spot, his eyes wide, his ears practically twitching with excitement. Screaming usually meant only one thing – adventure!

In the room below, Ben's uncle Tavish took a break from loading the supper plates into his latest invention – a heavy iron and brass cube he called the Automated Plate and Cup Washing Device – and shot Ben a stern look.

"Don't even think about it. It's bedtime!" he said.

"Come on, Uncle Tavish, just a quick peek," pleaded Ben, as a sudden crash from outside was followed by another burst of screaming. Ben hopped on to the handrail of the spiral metal staircase and slid all the way to the bottom.

By the time he jumped off, Ben was gripping his sword. The weapon may only have been made of wood, but he could still do some real damage with it. At least, he hoped so. He'd only built it that morning, and hadn't yet had a chance to put it to the test.

"Well ... fine. If you must," said Tavish. His mechanical arm whirred and a metal finger pointed Ben's way. "You can look. Nothing more. But if it's a giant I want you straight back in here," the blacksmith warned.

"Aw, but Uncle Tavish..."

"No buts, Benjamin," said Tavish, and Ben knew there was no point in arguing. Tavish only ever called him "Benjamin" when he was being serious. "I'm not having you out fighting giants. Not on a school night."

Ben mumbled his agreement, then twisted the brass handle and pushed open the wooden door that led outside. He bounded on to the main street of the village of Lump, his sword raised and ready. Ben skidded to a stop and gasped in surprise. For there, right

THE SWIVEL-EYED OGRE-Thing

in front of him was...

Nothing at all. The street was deserted. The screaming had stopped. An eerie stillness had fallen across the village.

Ben glanced along the street in both directions. Lump had grown a lot in the past month, ever since the neighbouring village of Loosh had been destroyed and everyone from

there had come to live here. Wooden huts now lined Lump's wide streets, providing temporary shelter for the Looshers until their own homes could be rebuilt.

The huts creaked softly in the breeze as Ben tiptoed past. Night had fallen, and the only light came from the faint shimmer of the half-moon, and the few torches flickering here and there on the walls of nearby houses.

"Hello?" said Ben, and his voice floated off into the dark. He could hear the horses whinny and neigh over in the stables, but otherwise all was silent. He scratched his head and slid his sword back into the belt of his tunic. Whatever the screaming had been about, it all seemed to have calmed down now.

"Huh," he sighed. "Well that wasn't as much fun as I expected."

He turned back towards his house, and that was when he saw it. Not a giant but

THE SWIVEL-EYED OGRE-THING

something else, emerging slowly from the shadows between two houses.

It crept along the street on all fours, its broad shoulders hunched, its curved horns lowered and pointing his way. Its breath swirled like steam through its flared nostrils, and its black hooves trip-trapped on the uneven surface of the road.

"Hey, a goat," said Ben, and he took a step towards the animal.

MEHHH!

With an angry bleat the goat charged. It thundered forwards, all hooves and horns and wild, wiry hair. Ben hurled himself sideways with scant seconds to spare. The goat trampled past, bucking and twisting as it skidded to a stop. Ben rolled to his feet and held his hands out in front of him.

"Nice goaty," he soothed. "Good goaty."

But the animal wasn't buying it. Lowering its head again it bounded towards him. It was fast. Much faster than Ben. He hammered on the door of the closest hut as the goat's hooves chewed up the distance between them.

"Hello?" he cried. "Anyone home? I'd really

THE SWIVEL-Eyed OGRE-Thing

like to come in, please!"

No one answered. The goat was almost on him now. Ben tried the door handle. Locked. Just his luck.

"Up here," called a familiar voice. Ben glanced up to see a small girl in a forest-green tunic reaching down to him. He caught her hand and scrambled up on to the roof. Below him, the goat hit the door like a battering ram, smashing it from its hinges and making the whole hut tremble and shake.

The goat barrelled through the open doorway and disappeared out of sight. From up on the roof, Ben heard it bleat with rage as it kicked and butted the inside of the hut to pieces.

Ben looked across to the girl who had helped him. Paradise Little was so short Ben had once

mistaken her for an elf. She was skinny, too, but Ben knew she was still pretty tough. For a girl, at least.

"Saved your life," she gloated.

"I had everything under control," Ben insisted.

Paradise gave a snort. "Yeah, right. If I hadn't grabbed you you'd have been a pancake."

Ben decided it probably wasn't the best time to get into an argument. "So where is everyone?" he asked. "Actually, let me guess. Hiding."

If the people of Lump were good at anything, they were good at hiding. Whenever danger reared its ugly head, you could always rely on the Lumpites to run screaming in the opposite direction, then barricade themselves safely

THE SWIVEL-EYED OGRE-Thing

out of harm's way.

There was a smash of breaking wood from below and the hut gave another shake. "What about Bibbly Codd?" Ben asked.

"About half a mile that way," said Paradise, who had an amazing knack of knowing where things were. She pointed along one of the paths leading away from Lump. "And getting further every second."

"He's making a run for it? I thought he was a goat tamer?"

"He is," Paradise said. "He's just a rubbish one."

"Great, so what do we do now then?"

"I suggest we stay up here," called another voice from nearby. "A goat's life expectancy is only around fifteen years. It'll die of old age

11

long before we do."

Ben looked over to where a boy in a red robe had tied himself to another roof with a length of rope. Like Paradise, Wesley Chant was new in town. The three of them had quickly become friends, even though Ben and Paradise spent half the time pretending they weren't.

THE SWIVEL-EYed OGRE-Thing

Wesley was a trainee wizard. At least he used to be, until he was kicked out of wizard school for having less magical ability than a sandwich.

"You're not seriously suggesting we stay up here for fifteen years?" Paradise said.

"Don't be ridiculous. Of course not!" replied Wesley. "I mean, that thing must be pushing a decade already. We shouldn't be up here for more than five years. Six tops."

"Well, I suppose it'd mean we'd miss school tomorrow," said Ben, then a sudden snap from below made the hut lurch sharply to one side. Paradise let out a yelp as she began to slip. Ben grabbed for her. His fingers brushed against hers, but then she was gone. She tumbled from the roof just as the goat butted its way through

the flimsy wooden wall. It stood there, its eyes
locked on her, its breath coming out in angry
snorts.

"Um, hi," she said. Then she ran. From the
safety of his rooftop, Wesley watched her go.

"Oh, that is a shame," he said. "I'm going to
miss her."

"You might, but the goat won't," said Ben.
"We've got to help her."

Wesley groaned. "I knew you were going to
say that."

With a well-aimed leap, Ben landed on the
goat's broad back. It bucked like a bronco and
kicked with its hind legs, forcing Ben to hold
on to its deadly horns.

"Now," he said, "we can either do this the
easy way, or the hard waaaaaaaaaaay!"

THE SWIVEL-Eyed OGRE-Thing

The goat rocketed forwards, throwing Ben's legs out behind him. Ben clung tightly to the animal's horns as it dragged him along, tossing and flicking him this way and that.

"Oh no, you couldn't have just chosen the easy way, could you?" Ben cried.

Up ahead, Paradise did her best to dodge, but the goat was already hot on her heels, hissing and panting like one of Tavish's steam-powered inventions. Her boot found a rock and she fell hard. The goat thundered towards her.

Muscles straining, Ben dragged himself up on to the animal's back. He dug his knees into its ribs and yanked hard on a horn. With an angry cry the goat veered sharply right. Ben looked up to see his own front door looming dead ahead of them, too close to stop or turn away.

"Right, Ben, time to come in," called Tavish, opening the door at just the wrong moment. He stopped and stared when he saw the goat hurtling towards him, Ben bouncing along on its back.

"Just coming!" bellowed Ben. Uncle Tavish leapt back as the goat charged past into the house.

CLANG! It hit the Automated Plate and Cup Washing Device head-on and came to a sudden crunching halt.

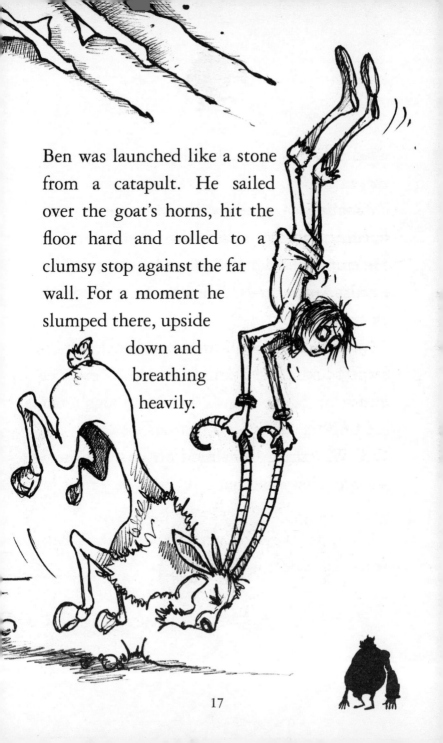

Ben was launched like a stone from a catapult. He sailed over the goat's horns, hit the floor hard and rolled to a clumsy stop against the far wall. For a moment he slumped there, upside down and breathing heavily.

17

Ben looked across to the goat, which now lay unconscious on his living-room floor. He looked up at Uncle Tavish, who was also staring at the goat, wondering where it had come from and why it had taken such a dislike to his Automated Plate and Cup Washing Device.

Grinning, Ben flipped himself over, got to his feet and dusted himself down. "Wow," he breathed. "School nights don't get much more exciting than that!"

"Troll!" cried a panicky voice from somewhere outside. "Run for your lives, there's a troll in the village!"

Ben's eyes widened with excitement. "Then again," he said, "maybe they do."

chapter Two

Ben raced outside to find Wesley dangling upside down from the roof of his hut, the rope tangled around his foot. His robe had fallen over his head, revealing a pair of bright red underpants with silver moons and stars sewn on.

A dark figure around Ben's height, but much

broader across the shoulders, stood by the hut, peering up at the boy wizard. Wesley flailed around helplessly, flapping and squirming at the end of the rope.

"Help!" he cried, his voice muffled by the robe. "Don't let it eat me!"

Paradise dusted herself down and joined Ben outside his house. "First a goat and then a troll," she said. "What's next? A Shark-Headed Bear-Thing?"

"Nah, already taken care of them," Ben said. He turned to her and grinned. "Oh, and by the way ... saved your life," he said, then he drew his wooden sword and hurried in the direction of the troll.

As they approached, the troll spun to face them. Its whole body was covered in bristly

THE SWIVEL-EYED OGRE-THING

black hair, and its yellow eyes narrowed as it spotted them. "Here," it said. "I know you. You were the ones what ruined my bridge, weren't you?"

Ben glanced at Paradise. He was no expert on trolls, but this one did look awfully familiar. "Um ... might have been," he admitted.

"It was," growled the troll, lumbering closer. He jabbed a clawed thumb in Wesley's direction. "It was you two an' him what done it. That was my bridge an' you snapped it clean in half!"

"Well, yes, but—"

The troll cracked its knuckles. "Then you legged it without playing Fart or Death."

"Because it's a ridiculous game," Paradise pointed out.

"It is not, it's brilliant!" the troll argued.

"You see," explained Ben, "these monsters had kidnapped the mayor and—"

The troll held up a finger to silence him, then opened its arms wide. Ben's hand tightened on his sword, but then he realised the creature was not moving to attack.

"Give us a hug," it said.

Ben blinked in surprise. "Um ... what?"

"Put it here. Don't be shy," urged the troll, beckoning Ben closer. "Get in for the real thing."

"I'm not sure..." began Ben, shifting uneasily. "I mean..."

"Oh just hug him!" wailed Wesley. "Before he gobbles us up."

THE SWIVEL-EYED OGRE-Thing

The troll stepped closer and pulled Ben in before he could resist. He squeezed, and Ben's nostrils were filled with a smell like rotten eggs.

"There you go," said the troll. "That's the way."

With a final squeeze he released Ben and stepped back. Paradise looked from one to the other and back again.

"So what was that about?" she asked.

"You three," the troll said, "saved my life."

"We did?" asked Paradise. "How?"

The troll glanced nervously into the darkness on either side. "Can we go inside first?" he asked. "It's not safe for me out here."

"Well you're not coming to my house. You'll stink the place up and leave hair everywhere," said Paradise.

"And it was destroyed by a goat," Ben reminded her.

Paradise groaned. "I'd forgotten about that."

"We'll go to mine," said Ben. "But if my uncle asks questions, leave the talking to me."

THE SWIVEL-EYED OGRE-Thing

He looked over to Wesley, who was still hanging upside down from the hut roof, his inside-out robe still draped over his head. "You coming, Wes?"

"What, with the troll?" he spluttered. "N-no, I think I'll just stay here."

"You sure? It looks a bit ... uncomfortable."

"What, this? No, it's great! I'm loving it," Wesley insisted. "I might start dangling upside down by one leg more often. It's surprisingly comfortable. You go, don't mind me!"

"I'll come back and cut you down in a minute," Ben promised.

"No rush!" said Wesley. "In your own time. Just you go."

Silence followed.

"Don't you worry about me at all!"

More silence.

"Oh," said Wesley. "You've already gone, haven't you?"

And they had.

The troll gave a low whistle. "Nice goat," he said, as Ben led him and Paradise into the house. "Had it long?"

"Just a few minutes," said Ben. "Bit worried what might happen when it wakes up."

"Won't wake up for hours yet," said the troll.

"How do you know?" asked Paradise.

"Trust me. One thing what I know about is goats. I'm an expert on 'em. After all, I am a tro—"

"Uncle Tavish!" said Ben, cutting the troll short just as the blacksmith's head popped up

THE SWIVEL-Eyed OGRE-Thing

from behind the Automated Plate and Cup Washing Device. "I'd like you to meet a friend of mine. This is... Um..."

"Scumbo," said the troll.

"Scumbo?" said Ben. "Seriously?"

"What's wrong with 'Scumbo'?" asked the troll, sounding slightly offended. "Issa good old-fashioned tro—"

"Trophy!" cried Ben. He forced a laugh. "A good old-fashioned trophy name, is what he was about to say. The, er, the kind of name that would look great on trophies."

"That's terrible," whispered Paradise.

"Shut up," muttered Ben. "I'm doing my best."

Tavish looked long and hard at Scumbo, then he looked at Ben. "Benjamin," he said.

"Is that a troll?"

"Yes," said Scumbo.

"No!" said Ben. "Haha. Oh Scumbo ... you kidder. No, of course it's not a troll. I know you'd never let me bring a troll into the house." He shot Scumbo a meaningful look.

"He just has ... an unfortunate medical condition," said Paradise.

"That makes him all hairy," said Ben.

"And troll-like," added Paradise.

THE SWIVEL-EYED OGRE-Thing

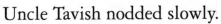

"It's a tragedy, really," Ben added. He lowered his voice. "Probably best not to talk about it."

Uncle Tavish nodded slowly.

"Right," he said. "It's just that I heard someone shouting 'troll' a minute ago, and now you're here with someone who looks quite a lot like a troll. No offence, Scumbo."

"None taken."

"Have you ever actually seen a troll, Uncle Tavish?" Ben asked.

"Well ... no. At least, not in a long time," the blacksmith admitted.

"Brilliant! I mean... Oh, right. Well, they look nothing like him," Ben said. "They're really big and scary."

"Not all stunted and smelling like feet," Paradise added.

"Here, who you calling stunted?" Scumbo demanded. He raised an arm and took a big sniff of his own armpit. "And I don't smell

THE SWIVEL-EYED OGRE-Thing

like... Actually no, you're right, I smell like feet."

"And look at the state of his teeth!" added Paradise. She prised open Scumbo's lips and showed off a copper-coloured graveyard of tooth stumps. "Trolls have much better dental hygiene than that."

"Exactly! You know what they say about trolls' teeth," said Ben. He started to back away up the staircase, and gestured for the other two to follow suit.

"No," frowned Tavish. "I don't."

"Don't you? Well there's something for you to find out, then," said Ben, flashing his most innocent smile. "Wesley will know. Go ask him."

"But if he says anything about trolls," added

Paradise, "he's a filthy liar."

With that, she followed Ben up the spiral staircase, dragging Scumbo along behind her. The troll gave Tavish a friendly wave. "Kids, eh?" he said, then he vanished through the hole leading to Ben's bedroom and the hatch closed over with a slam.

chapter Three

"Right, now spill," said Paradise. "How did we save your life?"

"And what are you so scared of?" added Ben.

Ben's bedroom was tucked up in the attic of the house, right below the thatched roof. There were no windows, but Scumbo still glanced in all directions before he started to speak.

"Someone's been taking trolls," he said, his voice hushed.

"Who would do that?" asked Ben.

"And why?" said Paradise. "Why would anyone choose to be around a troll if they didn't have to be?"

"Dunno," Scumbo admitted. "It's a puzzler all right. But it's happenin'. I saw it with my own two eyes."

"What exactly did you see?" said Ben.

Scumbo leaned in. "No trolls, that's what I seen," he said. "No trolls nowhere. 'Cept me."

"Maybe they've gone on holiday," suggested Paradise. Her nose crinkled as she caught a whiff of Scumbo. "Or for a bath, with a bit of luck."

Scumbo shook his hairy head. "They been

THE SWIVEL-Eyed OGRE-Thing

pinched," he said. "Snatched away by some 'orrible troll-taker. Swiped right out from under their bridges the lot of 'em."

"Why weren't you taken then?" Ben asked.

"Well, 'cos I don't got a bridge no more, do I? You lot broke it. And if you hadn't done ... well, who knows where I'd be now?"

Scumbo plonked himself down on the end of Ben's bed. It shuddered violently and gave a loud creak of protest.

"Let's just say you're right, and that someone really is kidnapping trolls," said Paradise. "How is that our problem? If you ask me they deserve a medal."

"Paradise!" said Ben. "That's a bit harsh."

"No it isn't," Paradise insisted. "Trolls eat people."

"No we don't," Scumbo said.

Paradise frowned. "You do so! Back at the bridge you said—"

Scumbo stood up. The bed gave a squeak of relief. "Oh yeah, I mean we say we eat people. We say it all right, but how many people do you know what've ever actually been eaten by a troll?"

"Mr Asquith the baker had his arm bitten off by one," Paradise said.

THE SWIVEL-EYed OGRE-Thing

"Oh yeah, I mean – granted – we partly eat people. We partly eat 'em, yeah. I mean who doesn't partly eat—"

"And both legs."

"We mostly eat people, I'll give you," Scumbo said, after just a moment's hesitation. "We gobble up most of 'em, of course, but we don't fully eat 'em, that's the point I'm trying to make here. Beside, we provides a valuable public service, we do."

"Oh, don't talk rubbish," Paradise said. "What public service?"

"How many wild goats you had come trip-trappin' into town before tonight? Tearing the place up and scaring all the little kiddly-winks? Hmm? How many?"

Ben and Paradise exchanged a glance.

"Well … none," Ben admitted.

"That's 'cos of all us trolls guarding all them bridges," Scumbo said. "Stopping them goats getting past. Stopping other things, too. Worse things. Things so nasty they'll make your eyes burst just looking at 'em."

"What, like Paradise you mean?" asked Ben, then he jumped back to avoid a slap. "I'm kidding!"

"Yeah, you laugh while you can," said Scumbo, in a voice as solemn as the grave. "But without no trolls to guard them bridges, this whole place is gonna be neck-deep in nastiness before you can say 'I wish we'd helped out that nice Scumbo fella when we had the chance. He knew a thing or two, he did'."

"Help you?" Paradise said.

THE SWIVEL-EYED OGRE-Thing

"How?" said Ben.

"That mayor what you went looking for," said Scumbo. "Find him, did you?"

Ben nodded. "We did." He jabbed a thumb in Paradise's direction. "She can find anything."

"Then find them trolls. Find 'em, and find out who took 'em." The troll looked from Ben to Paradise and back again. "Or else one little angry goat is gonna be the least of your problems."

The cogs inside Tavish's mechanical arm whirred quietly as he reached up to scratch his head. Now he was really confused.

"So ... he *is* a troll?"

"Yes," said Ben.

"It came as a real surprise to all of us,"

39

said Paradise.

"'Cept me," Scumbo added.

"Yes. Except him."

"And you want to go with him to find some other trolls who've all been...?"

"Taken," said Ben.

"By...?"

"We don't know."

"For...?"

"We don't know that either."

Tavish frowned. "So ... let me get this straight. You want to go out in the dark with a man-eating creature to track down some other man-eating creatures who've all been kidnapped by someone—"

"Or something," added Scumbo.

"Thank you, yes. Or something which by

THE SWIVEL-EYED OGRE-THING

default must be even worse than they are, for reasons currently unknown." He leaned in to give the next part extra emphasis. "On a school night."

"That sounds about right," said Ben.

"It sounds a bit dangerous."

A voice from the doorway interjected before Ben could reply.

"Oh come now, Mr Tavish. It's nothing the great Benjamin Blank can't handle!"

They all turned to find the Mayor of Loosh filling the doorway.

He flashed them his polished smile and closed the gap between them with three determined strides. The mayor ruffled Paradise's hair. "Sorry I didn't wait for you when that goat attacked, my dear," he said. "I knew my safety would be your number one concern. And, of course, I knew you'd be perfectly fine."

"She was almost trampled," Ben said. The mayor turned his smile on him, and Ben felt his skin crawl. He might be the closest thing Paradise had to a dad, but there was something about the mayor that made Ben uneasy.

"Almost trampled is merely another way of saying not trampled," the mayor said. "And for that I'm eternally grateful."

"Who's the fatso?" asked Scumbo, peering up at the newcomer.

THE SWIVEL-Eyed OGRE-Thing

"He's not a fasto, he's the Mayor of Loosh," explained Tavish.

"Looks like a fatso to me." Scumbo's nostrils flared. "An' he smells funny."

"Ahaha. Charming," said the mayor, brushing off the insults. "Did I hear correctly, Mr ... Troll thing? Were you asking for young Benjamin's assistance?"

"He was, but it sounds dangerous," said Tavish.

The mayor rested a hand on Ben's shoulder. Ben tried to pull away, but the mayor was stronger than his flabby frame suggested. "Dangerous? For the boy who defeated the Shark-Headed Bear-Things and saved me from a fate worse than death? Nonsense! It's nothing he can't handle." He placed his other

43

hand on Paradise's shoulder. "Besides, he'd have my Paradise to help him find his way home."

Tavish didn't look convinced, but Ben could see it wouldn't take much to tip things in his favour. "Remember what the Soothsayer High Council told you?" he said. "This stuff – battling monsters – it's my destiny."

"Yes," said Tavish. "That's what I'm afraid of." He looked down at Ben and smiled sadly. "If I say no, will you go anyway?"

"Of course not!"

"Tell me the truth, Benjamin."

"Yes," Ben admitted. "Probably. Those trolls could be in trouble and, well, someone's got to help them, right? It's like you always told me. There's the easy thing to do and there's

THE SWIVEL-EYED OGRE-Thing

the right thing to do, and they aren't always the same. This is the right thing to do, Uncle Tavish. I can feel it."

"Oh, this boy," said the mayor, wiping an invisible tear from the corner of one eye. "This boy!"

Tavish sighed. Ben held his breath. Scumbo farted loudly.

"Sorry," he said. "Been hanging on to that for ages."

"Good grief," yelped Paradise, recoiling. "That's disgusting."

The smell hit Tavish and he stepped back. Even though an old cooking injury meant the blacksmith's nose was made almost entirely out of wood, the smell somehow still managed to find a way through.

"Right, go, go," he urged. "Go do what you have to do, and take that thing with you. Just please ... be careful."

"I will," Ben promised. He turned to Paradise and Scumbo. "You two go wait outside."

"Good. Fresh air!" wheezed Paradise, her voice muffled by a handkerchief she had pressed over her nose and mouth. She made a move towards the door, then stopped. "Wait, what about you?"

"I'd imagine Benjamin is going to get that wonderful glove of his," said the mayor. He

THE SWIVEL-EYED OGRE-Thing

smiled, showing too many teeth. "Isn't that right, Ben?"

"Uh ... yeah. That's right," said Ben, and he headed for a small door at the back of the room, with the mayor's gaze following him every step of the way.

Ben tiptoed down the rough stone stairs leading into the dark depths of the basement. It had only been a few weeks since he'd been running up them, a Shark-Headed Bear-Thing snapping at his heels. Since then he'd only been back once, and as the flickering torch in his hand sent shadows scurrying across the walls, he felt his heart begin to beat a little faster.

At last, he reached the bottom and stepped

down on to the hard-packed soil floor. The torchlight picked out two shapes tucked against one wall – a box, and something hidden beneath a faded old blanket. Beside them, a large hole in the wall had been barricaded with boulders and bits of scrap metal. Ben checked the barrier to make sure it was still secure, then made his way over to the box.

THE SWIVEL-EYED OGRE-Thing

He opened the lid and there, just where he'd left it, was the metal gauntlet. Tavish had given it to him before his encounter with the Bear-Things, but insisted Ben put it back after the adventure was over. It wasn't a toy, Tavish had said, but Ben wouldn't have dreamed of playing with it anyway. It had been one of two items found with Ben in the wreckage of an old wagon, back when Ben was just a baby, and that meant it was something much more important than a toy.

It was a clue. A clue to his past, and to what had happened to his parents.

He slipped the metal glove over his right hand and felt a brief tingle travel along his fingertips. According to Tavish's Automated Magic Detecting Device, the gauntlet was packed with magical power. Unfortunately, Ben hadn't quite figured out how to use it properly. Still, just by wearing it he felt braver somehow, like there was no challenge he couldn't face.

And speaking of challenges...

Ben turned to the blanket. He pulled it away, revealing the second object that had been found alongside him in that wreckage. The handle of a sword stuck up from a lump of heavy rock. The blade was buried deep in

THE SWIVEL-EYED OGRE-Thing

the stone, with only a few centimetres of the polished steel showing. A symbol in the shape of a clawed creature was embossed on the weapon's hilt. Its eyes seemed to follow Ben as he reached out and took hold of the handle.

"I'm ready," he whispered into the darkness. "This is my sword, and I'm ready."

He pulled. His grip slipped off the handle. He took hold and tried again.

"I'm ready," he said, more loudly this time. "Come ... out!"

But the sword stayed stuck in the stone, no matter how hard he pulled.

Releasing his grip, Ben let out a sigh. "Oh well," he said, looking down at the wooden sword stuck in the belt of his tunic. "Looks like you're just going to have to do."

Chapter Four

Wesley hit the ground with a thud. He bounced to his feet, the robe still tangled above his head. For a moment he just ran in circles screaming at the top of his voice, then he turned too sharply and smacked straight into the side of his hut.

"Oof!" he yelped. He wrestled his clothing

THE SWIVEL-EYED OGRE-Thing

back into place, saw a troll smiling at him, then tried to run away again. Paradise caught him by the back of the robe and spun him around to face her.

"Wesley," she snapped. "Calm down."

"Troll!" Wesley cried, pointing frantically in case Paradise had somehow missed the hairy monster standing beside her. "The t-troll's here."

"I know," Paradise said. "Don't worry about it. We're going to help him."

"Help him? Are you mad?"

Paradise shrugged. "Believe me, it wasn't my idea."

Wesley's mouth dropped open. His eyes went wide as he gawped at the troll, then back to Paradise. "Ben?"

"Ben," she confirmed.

"What about me?" asked Ben, trotting up to join them.

"They said you're a maniac," Scumbo explained.

THE SWIVEL-EYED OGRE-Thing

"No we didn't," spluttered Wesley.

"Well, not in so many words, maybe," admitted Scumbo. "But that was the general idea. They don't reckon you should be helping me. They's a couple of troll haters."

"I don't hate trolls," Wesley said. "I'm terrified of them."

Scumbo smiled knowingly. "Aha! You's only scared because you don't understand us."

"And because you might eat me!"

"Mostly eat you," Scumbo corrected. "Not all the way. An' I'm not going to eat no one." He winked in Wesley's direction. "Not right now, anyway."

"Someone's kidnapping trolls," Ben explained. "We're going to help find them."

"I'm not coming!" Wesley said, a little more

high-pitched than he'd intended. He cleared his throat. "I mean, you know ... fun as it sounds. I'll just stay here and, um, keep an eye on things. Just you go on without me."

Ben nodded. "Good idea."

This took Wesley by surprise. "Is it?"

"Yeah," said Ben. "You can help defend the village. Without the trolls to guard the bridges there's no saying what might be on its way here even now. More goats, maybe."

"Or goblins," said Scumbo. "Nasty little bleeders, goblins."

"G-goblins?"

"Don't forget the ogres. You do know how to fight an ogre, don't you?" Paradise said. "Don't let it rip your legs off. That's step one."

Wesley's face had turned a grim shade of

THE SWIVEL-EYED OGRE-THING

grey. He peered into the gloom surrounding the village and his whole body spasmed with fear.

"On s-second thoughts," he said, "you might need my assistance. With magic and information and whatnot."

Ben stroked his chin. "I dunno..."

"Please let me come!" Wesley squeaked. "Don't leave me here with the ogres."

"And goblins," Scumbo reminded him.

Wesley whimpered. "Or them."

"Well ... OK," said Ben. "You've twisted my arm. You can come."

"Oh, thank you!" said Wesley. He glanced nervously at every shadow, as if something might lunge out at any moment. "I suggest we leave right away."

"Good idea." Ben turned to Paradise. "Right then, do your stuff."

Paradise frowned. "What?"

"Your findy thing. Find us a troll."

Paradise extended an arm and pointed in Scumbo's direction. "Found one."

Ben folded his arms. "Very funny."

"I'm not joking," replied Paradise. "My power doesn't work like that. You can't just say 'find a troll' and then expect me to find one."

"Why not?"

"Because there's a troll there!" said Paradise, pointing to Scumbo again. "If I try to find a troll, I'm just going to keep finding him. I need something connected to one of the missing ones. Something specific."

THE SWIVEL-EYed OGRE-Thing

She turned to Scumbo. "Do you have a picture of one of the lost trolls?"

"No."

"Do you have anything belonging to them?"

"No."

"Do you have, I don't know, a lock of their back hair or something?"

"Yes!" said Scumbo.

"That's great!" said Paradise. "And completely revolting."

"Actually wait ... I don't," said the troll. "Misunderstood the question. Sorry."

Paradise tutted. "Then I can't find them."

Ben frowned. "I don't get it. You didn't have anything of mine. How did you find me?"

"Unlucky, I guess," Paradise said with a smirk. "With you I was looking for someone

59

who could help. Had some big brave hero type been standing next to me, I'd have found him. There wasn't, so I found you."

Ben's frown deepened. "I don't get it."

"Why doesn't that surprise me?" Paradise sighed. "If I look for a hero, I'll find the closest hero – in that case, you. If I look for a troll, I'll find the closest troll – in this case, him."

She jabbed a thumb in Scumbo's direction.

THE SWIVEL-EYed OGRE-Thing

He gave a little wave.

"If you want me to find a particular troll, then you have to give me something to work with, otherwise I'm going to keep coming back to the stinkbeast here."

Wesley let out a yelp. "Wait! That's it!"

He reached a hand up inside one of his baggy sleeves and fished out a large leather-bound book.

He hurriedly flipped through the pages. "Lunt Bingwood wrote something..."

"What's a Lunt Bingwood?" asked Scumbo.

"He's the greatest adventurer who ever lived," replied Ben. He had only heard about Lunt Bingwood recently, but already the tales of the adventurer-turned-author had made a big impression. It was a shame he had mysteriously disappeared shortly after writing his book. Ben would have loved to have met him and swapped adventure stories.

"He wrote this monster guide book," said Wesley, holding up the hefty tome. "Who's Who, What's What, and Why They Do Such Horrible Things to One Another." Wesley flicked on a few more pages then stopped. "Aha, here it is! According to Lunt Bingwood,

THE SWIVEL-EYed OGRE-Thing

all trolls have their own unique scent."

"You're not wrong there," agreed Scumbo.

Wesley closed the book and shoved it back up his sleeve. "Paradise could use those unique odours to find the missing trolls!"

Ben stifled a laugh. "Like a dog you mean?"

"Oi, watch it," Paradise warned, shooting him one of her scary looks. She shrugged. "I suppose it might work."

"Then all we have to do is find a sample of their scent," Wesley said.

"And where are we going to find that?" asked Paradise.

Scumbo realised they were all staring at him. "What you looking at me for? How'm I supposed to know?"

Paradise rolled her eyes and sighed. "Because

you're a troll."

"Oh," said Scumbo. "Yeah. Fair point."

"Doesn't matter. I know where to go," announced Ben. He took a torch from a nearby wall and held it out to light the way. "Paradise, find us a bridge!"

The four figures trudged along through the dark, tripping and stumbling on the uneven ground. The moon had long since ducked behind the summit of Mount Nochance, the most imposing mountain in all the four kingdoms.

The mountain was so named because "no chance" was usually the first thing anyone said if someone suggested climbing it. Even the most hardened of explorers would take one

THE SWIVEL-EYED OGRE-Thing

look at its craggy slopes and cloud-covered peak, then immediately develop a nosebleed and remember they really had to be somewhere else.

Over the centuries a few brave souls had summoned the courage to begin the long climb to the top, but none – as of yet – had ever come back down again. At least, not without making a messy splat at the bottom.

Wesley walked at Ben's side, so close that their shoulders were practically touching. He was startled by every sound beyond the circle of light cast by the flame of the torch, and Ben could feel him jump with every noise they heard.

Whooo!

"What was that?"

"An owl," said Ben.

Chirp-chirp-chirp!

"Crickets," Ben said, before Wesley could even ask.

RAAAAAAR!

"What was that one?" Wesley yelped.

"No idea," Ben admitted.

THE SWIVEL-EYED OGRE-THING

"Sorry," said Paradise. "That was me. Couldn't resist."

Wesley gasped. "That's just cruel!"

"How much further is it?" asked Ben. He'd been right up for an adventure, but as adventures went this one had been really boring so far.

"We've only been walking for ten minutes," Paradise said. "And that's the third time you've asked that."

"Is that all?" Ben groaned. He trudged on a few more paces. "How much further is it?"

Paradise shook her head. "Not far. We're nearly at Bibkin's Trickle."

"What's Bibkin's Trickle?" asked Ben.

"Oh no. It's a monster, isn't it,"

whimpered Wesley. "It's a horrible big monster that will—"

"It's a stream," Paradise said. "With a bridge over it."

Wesley let out a sigh of relief. "Oh, *that* Bibkin's Trickle," he said, then he stopped abruptly.

"What's up?" asked Ben.

"Sssh!"

Paradise sighed. "What've you heard now? A man-eating badger? A killer squirrel?"

"Don't. Move. A muscle," Wesley whispered, and there was something in his voice that made the others stand up straight and pay attention.

Ben brought the torch closer to Wesley's face. The wizard looked in a state of mild panic most of the time, but now his expression was

THE SWIVEL-EYED OGRE-Thing

like a mask of pure fear. His eyes darted across the ground ahead of them. Despite the cool night air, a bead of sweat trickled down his forehead and dripped from the end of his nose.

"What is it?" asked Ben. "What's wrong?"

"G-give me the torch," Wesley whispered. He took it from Ben and bent low, slowly sweeping the flickering glow across the road ahead. Down near the ground at the very edge of the light's circle, two bulging red eyes reflected back at them.

Ribbit.

"It's a frog," said Paradise flatly.

"You nearly gave me a flamin' heart attack!" gasped Scumbo.

"N-not a frog," Wesley whimpered. "It's a t-toad."

"Are you getting toads mixed up with something else?" Paradise wondered. "Like bears or tigers or something? I mean, they're not exactly terrifying."

While Paradise had been talking, Wesley had carefully lifted a small stone from the ground. With a flick of his wrist he tossed it towards the toad. It bounced off its head with a faint *plink*.

A second later, the toad exploded. It went off like a bomb blast, spraying fire and guts in all directions at once. A chunk of slimy leg splattered across Paradise's face, and the force of the bang knocked all four of them backwards off their feet.

Once the smoke had cleared Paradise looked shakily across at the others. "That whole not

terrifying thing. Is it too late to take that back?"

chapter Five

Ben helped the others to their feet. "You've got toad on you," he told Paradise. She pulled the leg off her forehead with a gloopy schlop, then shuddered in disgust.

"An Explodi-Toad!" said Wesley. "I knew it. They blow up at the slightest touch."

"So you thought you'd chuck a rock at it,"

THE SWIVEL-EYed OGRE-Thing

said Paradise. "Genius plan, Wesley."

"I had to be sure," Wesley whispered. "Because, well you see, the thing is..."

He inched forwards and held the torch out before him. Dozens of little eyes reflected back at them through the gloom.

Ribbit.

Ribbit.

Ribbit.

"Explodi-Toads never travel alone."

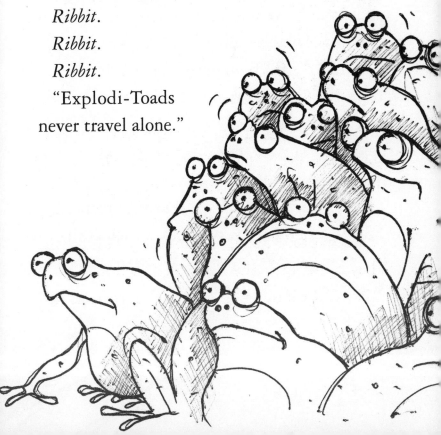

Ben nodded. "So we just avoid touching any more of them and we should be fine, right?"

He took a few careful steps along the path, but Wesley grabbed him before he could go any further.

"No!" the wizard warned. "You don't understand. They're rarely seen out in the open like this. They usually live underground."

"And...?" said Ben, not understanding.

"Just a few centimetres underground to be exact," Wesley continued. "They hide right below the surface, out of sight. If you step on one..."

"Then it's bye-bye Ben," Paradise realised.

"If it sets off a chain reaction then it's bye-bye all of us," Wesley said. "We have no choice. We have to turn back."

THE SWIVEL-EYED OGRE-Thing

"We'll find another way around then," Ben agreed. They all turned, slowly and carefully. Several more sets of eyes blinked at them from the darkness up ahead.

Ribbit.

Ribbit.

Ribbit.

"Right, so that'll be us surrounded then," realised Ben. "Anyone got any ideas?"

"We stand here and don't move," suggested Wesley.

"For how long?"

Wesley chewed a fingernail. "Forever?"

"I'm standing downwind of Scumbo," Paradise pointed out. "There's no way I'm standing here forever. What about your glove?"

Ben looked down at the gauntlet. The

flickering torchlight made the metal look alive. "What about it?"

"Can't you summon up a portal that'll suck all these things through?"

"I suppose I could try," said Ben. "If you don't mind having dozens of exploding toads come flying past your head at a hundred miles an hour."

"What about you?" Scumbo grunted at Wesley. "You're a wizard, aren't you? Can't you magic them away?"

"P-probably not," Wesley confessed. "I've tried to use magic to help us in the past."

"He tried to fight off a pack of monsters," Paradise said. "But instead he made custard."

"Quite a small amount," Ben added.

"Well I'd like to see either of you two make

THE SWIVEL-EyED OGRE-Thing

custard out of thin air," Wesley sniffed.

"I've never had custard," said Scumbo. "What's it like?"

"Not bad, actually," said Wesley. "If you make it right it's quite creamy and—"

"Is this really the best time to discuss desserts?" asked Paradise. She waited until she was sure they'd stopped talking, then turned and pointed to a spot on the ground around ten metres ahead of them. "There's one there," she said. "We can go around it, then there's another one a bit further up on the left."

"You're not going to try to go through them!" Wesley gasped.

"I can find a safe path," Paradise said. "I can find anything."

"But one false step and we go boom!"

"Well you'd better not make a false step, then."

"Are those two the closest ones?" asked Ben, stepping between his friends. Paradise nodded.

"Right then," Ben said, scooping up a handful of gravel, "we can just do this."

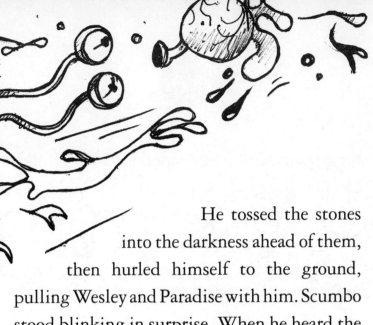

He tossed the stones into the darkness ahead of them, then hurled himself to the ground, pulling Wesley and Paradise with him. Scumbo stood blinking in surprise. When he heard the gravel rain down he clamped his hands over his ears, yelped in panic, and dropped like a sack of potatoes.

KA-BA-BOOOOM!

It wasn't an explosion exactly. It was more like an eruption, as if the world itself were suddenly vomiting up flame and rock and soggy lumps of smouldering toad. The noise was like nothing they had ever heard. It shook their teeth and rattled their bones and filled their heads with its thunder. Pebbles fell like hailstones around them, quickly followed by a heavy downpour of warm amphibian guts.

When the world was still again, they all stood up shakily. They took a moment to scoop the toady mush from their ears, and flick the worst of it out of their hair, before any of them finally spoke.

"You maniac!" cried Paradise. "You almost blew us all to pieces!"

Ben grinned. "Almost blew us all to pieces is just another way of saying didn't blow us all to pieces," he said. "Any left?"

Paradise shook her head in disbelief, then turned and pointed somewhere off to their left. "One or two that way," she said. "But the bridge is over in that direction."

THE SWIVEL-EYED OGRE-Thing

"Nice one," said Ben. "Lead the way!"

Through everything, the torch had somehow managed to stay lit. Paradise took it, then set off across the gut-drenched, pot-holed ground. Ben followed, with Wesley and Scumbo slipping and sliding through the gutty mush behind him.

"So," said Scumbo, flicking a tiny toad eyeball off Wesley's shoulder. "What was that you was sayin' about custard?"

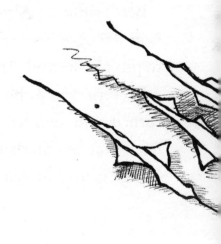

Chapter Six

As they approached the bridge, Ben wondered if it had been worth all the bother. It was barely three metres long, and had been thrown together out of old wood and bits of scrap metal. The bridge was more or less hump-backed – higher in the middle than it was at the ends – but it leaned heavily to one side,

THE SWIVEL-EYED OGRE-Thing

as if threatening to throw itself into the water below. There was barely a breath of wind, and yet the bridge creaked and groaned like it was being battered by a hurricane.

"There she is," breathed Scumbo, his yellow eyes sweeping across the misshapen planks. "What a beauty. Have you ever seen anything like it?"

"No," said Ben, with absolute honesty. "I have never seen anything like that."

There were four unlit torches attached to four metal poles near the bridge. Ben used his own flame to light them, and Wesley visibly relaxed as a widening circle of light pushed away the darkness. Wesley glanced at the bridge, then glanced at it again, as if not quite believing what he'd seen the first time.

"What a dump," said Paradise.

"Well now, I wouldn't call it a dump," said Wesley.

"What would you call it, then?"

Wesley studied the bridge again. "A deathtrap?" he ventured, after some consideration.

"There's nothing wrong with it!" protested Scumbo. "Solid as a rock this." He shook one of the handrails to prove his point. It immediately fell off and plunged into the stream. They all watched it float off until it was lost to the dark. Scumbo cleared his throat. "That bit's meant to do that," he said, then he slowly backed away and rejoined the others.

Reassured by the torchlight, and by the glow of the moon that had once more popped out

THE SWIVEL-EYED OGRE-Thing

from behind Mount Nochance, Wesley began to explore. He ventured down to the edge of the stream and watched the water babble on by. "So this is Bibkin's Trickle," he said. "You know, some experts believe it might have been named after someone called 'Bibkin'."

"Really?" yawned Paradise.

"Yes indeed," Wesley continued. "Although there's some debate over it."

"That's fascinating stuff," Paradise said.

"It is, isn't it?" Wesley agreed. "Some believe that 'Bibkin' was in fact an old word meaning 'brook' or 'stream' and that actually someone named 'Trickle' may be responsible for the naming—"

"Goblin!" cried Paradise.

With a yelp, Wesley came hareing up the

bank and leapt into Ben's arms. "Wh-where?"

Paradise fought back a smirk. "Oh no. False alarm," she said, as innocently as she could.

Ben set Wesley down, then strode over to the bridge and peeked beneath it. There was a narrow space just a metre or so wide between the start of the bridge and the edge of the water. Peering in, Ben could see a rumpled blanket in there, half-buried in the mud. It was the only sign that anyone had ever been living there.

"Definitely no troll," he said. "Just an old blanket."

He ducked lower and began to clamber into the gap. "You're not seriously going in there!" gasped Wesley. "It might be dangerous."

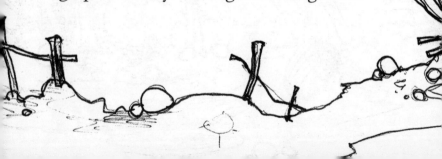

THE SWIVEL-EYED OGRE-Thing

"It's OK, Wes. I'm pretty sure I can handle a blanket."

"Although you did get knocked unconscious by a slice of toast last month," Paradise reminded him. She smiled sweetly. "Just saying."

Ben ducked into the shadows beneath the bridge and Paradise followed. Scumbo stuck close to them, leaving Wesley to quickly

squeeze in behind the troll. "Don't leave me out there by myself," he said, before a cheeky parp from Scumbo forced him back.

"You really need to see someone about that," Paradise wheezed, pulling the neck of her tunic up to cover her mouth.

"Nah, we're all a bit on the gassy side, us trolls," Scumbo said, and he sounded quite proud of the fact. "What's really special about a troll guff is it's lighter than air, so it always wafts gently upwards into the nostrils."

Paradise coughed and wiped tears from her eyes. "I think both mine just melted."

Ben squatted down and examined the blanket. It was soaking wet and caked with slippery mud. "Looks like the water got to it," he said.

THE SWIVEL-EYED OGRE-Thing

"Great," sighed Paradise, pinching her nose. "So between the stream washing the scent away and him farting the place up, there's no trail for me to follow."

"Can't you get some sort of reading off the blanket or something?"

Paradise looked doubtful, but held out a hand. "Give it here and I'll try."

Ben dragged the blanket out of the mud and passed it to her. Dirty water drizzled from it and dribbled its way back into Bibkin's Trickle. On the ground, right where the blanket had been, Ben spotted a shape pressed into the mud. He studied it from all angles, trying to figure out what it was.

It was a large sort of triangle shape, with four knobbly ovals up near the widest end.

Each oval was larger than the one on its left, and Ben couldn't shake the feeling that there was something strangely familiar about the outline.

"Nothing," said Paradise. "The water's washed it clean. I'm not getting anything from it."

"Look at this," said Ben. Paradise and Scumbo joined him in staring down at the imprint.

"Cor," said Scumbo. "That's big, innit?"

"What is it?" asked Paradise.

Slowly, Ben looked from the shape to his own left foot. Without a word, he placed his heel into the pointy end of the triangle. The tip of his boot barely reached a quarter of the way along to the ovals, which he now

THE SWIVEL-EyeD OGRE-Thing

knew had to be toes.

Wesley's head popped up over Scumbo's shoulder. "What we looking at?" he asked, then he spotted the footprint in the mud.

"Must've been one big troll," Ben whispered.

Scumbo shook his head. "That ain't no troll footprint," he said. "Trolls only got three toes."

It was Paradise who eventually asked the question that was on all their minds. "So what is it?"

"Whatever took the trolls must have made it," Ben said. He turned to Wesley. "Any ideas?"

Wesley puffed out his cheeks. "Run away screaming?" he suggested.

"I meant any ideas on what made that?"

"Yes!" Wesley yelped. "Something massive and terrifying that will almost certainly kill us."

Ben looked to Paradise. "Can you find whatever made this footprint?"

THE SWIVEL-EYED OGRE-Thing

"Please say no," Wesley squeaked.

Paradise shifted uncomfortably. "I'm not sure I really want to," she said, but she edged past Ben and knelt down in the mud. Her fingers traced the contours of the footprint and her eyes closed over. A frown flickered across her brow as she tried to get a lock on the owner of that foot.

"Anything?"

"I don't ... I'm not ... maybe," Paradise said. Her forehead furrowed as she concentrated harder. "I'm picking up something, it's just..."

"What?"

"It's just, I don't know. It's moving fast. Really fast."

"Yeah, that doesn't help us at all," said Ben. "We need to know where it is."

"Give me a minute!" Paradise said. She focused, and groaned with the effort. "It's..."

Ben leaned in. "Yes?"

"It's..."

"Yes?"

Paradise's eyes flicked wide. She stared, first at Ben, then at the footprint. "Oh no," she said, in a voice that could barely be heard above the babbling of the stream.

"What's the matter?" asked Ben. "Where is it?"

Paradise swallowed. "It's... It's..."

BADOOM! With a sound not unlike an exploding Explodi-Toad, the whole bridge shuddered. Paradise raised one

THE SWIVEL-EYED OGRE-Thing

finger and pointed to the rotten wood above their heads.

"It's right up there!"

chapter Seven

"TROLL!"

Barely ten minutes before, the sound of several dozen toads being blown to smithereens had been the loudest sound Ben had ever heard. That record had just been broken by the voice of the thing up on the bridge. It boomed like a twenty-one cannon salute. Ben clamped his

THE SWIVEL-EYED OGRE-Thing

hands over his ears to block out the din, and almost punched himself to the ground with the metal gauntlet.

"GET YOU UP HERE, TROLL!" roared the voice. "YOU DONE LIT YOUR LAMPS, I KNOWS YOU'S HERE!"

"Goodness me," whispered Wesley. "His grammar's terrible." The others stared at him. "S-sorry. Coping strategy," he explained. "I'm hoping if I focus on the little things it'll stop my head exploding in fear."

"I'S WARNING YOU, TROLL! GET YOU UP HERE!"

Wesley shook his head. "Call that sentence construction?" he whimpered, then he jammed his fist in his mouth and began to rock back and forth in the mud.

"I think you'd better go up," said Ben.

"I think you're right," agreed Scumbo, then he realised Ben was talking to him. "What, me?"

"Well of course you," Paradise hissed.

"You gotta be joking," Scumbo snorted. "Listen to him. He sounds mental. Anyway," he said, pointing to Ben, "he's the one what lit the lamps, not me."

"But I'm not a troll, am I?" said Ben.

Scumbo hesitated. "What? Um. Yeah, well … neither am I."

"Yes you are."

"All right, yes I am, obviously," Scumbo admitted. "But still. I can't go up there. That'll rip me to bits that will."

"It won't," Ben said. "We'll all be right

THE SWIVEL-EYED OGRE-THING

behind you."

"YOU DONE COMIN' UP HERE, TROLL?"

Wesley let out a near-hysterical laugh. "Really shocking grammar. Bet he's rubbish at sums as well."

"As far as we know it hasn't killed any trolls," Paradise said. "Just kidnapped them."

"Oh, well that makes me feel a lot better, that does," snapped Scumbo.

"You go up and distract him, then we'll hit him from behind," Ben urged. "We'll tie him up and make him tell us where the other trolls are."

"Or he'll bash my head in as soon as it pops up, then wear me like a scarf for the rest of his life."

"I won't let anything happen to you," Ben said. "I promise."

"I'S GOING TO COUNT TO FIVE, TROLL!"

"Oho," giggled Wesley. "This should be interesting."

"ONE!"

Scumbo looked down at the footprint in the mud. The massive footprint in the mud.

"TWO!"

The troll sighed. "All right, all right," he mumbled, shoving his way past Paradise. He looked back at Ben. "Right behind me?"

"Right behind you," Ben assured him.

"UM ... FOUR!"

Wesley squeaked with laughter. "Four he says!"

Scumbo ducked out
from beneath the bridge.
Ben and the others held their breath as they
heard the troll clamber up the wooden planks.
"I am a troll, fol-de-rol, and I'll eat you up
for..." he began, then his voice tailed off into
silence.

There was a creaking as Scumbo climbed
back down. He faced them in the shadows, his
eyes bulging with terror.

"I think we might have a problem," he said, then a hulking hand caught him by the head and yanked him out of sight.

"Now!" cried Ben, drawing his sword. He dashed out of the narrow space, with Paradise right at his heels.

"What, we're not really going to help are we?" Wesley yelped. "I thought that was all a trick so we could run away!"

The planks above him rattled sharply as if the whole bridge was about to come crashing down. Wesley squealed and scrabbled up the bank after Ben, who was already vaulting over the one remaining handrail, making straight for...

Straight for...

Ben stopped running.

THE SWIVEL-EYED OGRE-Thing

He looked up.

And up.

And up, until he finally found the face of the thing on the bridge. It was an ogre. Ben had never seen an ogre before, and he wasn't sure exactly how he knew that this was one. Everything about it just screamed OGRE though, from its bald head and pig-like snout, to its scarred muscles that bulged from armour made of polished bone.

And yet it wasn't just an ogre, it was something more. Or something less. One of its legs was a twisted tangle of brass and steel. Its bottom jaw was a grimace of polished metal, hinged on either side by two rusted cogs, and there was a round lens, like the end of a telescope, where one of the monster's eyes should have been.

Scumbo was dangling by a leg from one of the ogre's hands. He shot Ben a withering look as he rushed on to the bridge. "We'll jump him from behind, you said. I won't let anything happen to you, you said!"

Paradise and Wesley hung back, both frozen with fear. Ben felt his throat go dry as he slowly raised his wooden sword until it was pointing at the troll's head. "Let him go," he said. "This is your only warning."

"Oh, well that's got him quaking in his boots, that has," spat Scumbo. "An' here was me getting worried."

"LITTLE BUG FUNNY," boomed the ogre. There was a hiss and a cloud of steam as it raised its robotic leg and snapped it down

THE SWIVEL-EYED OGRE-Thing

towards Ben. Ben stumbled back as the planks at his feet exploded in a cloud of splinters and dust. The ogre's leg carried on right through the hole, throwing the brute off balance.

Ben saw his chance. With a roar he swung with his sword at the monster's real knee. There was a loud crack and Ben let out a cry of triumph. His excitement quickly faded when he realised the cracking sound had come from his sword, and not the ogre's leg. He looked down at the broken handle in his hand.

"Oh come on," he groaned. "Not again!"

The mechanical foot tore back up through the floor, and the whole bridge lurched violently to one side. Ben staggered, flailing frantically as he stumbled towards the waiting water. He grabbed for the first thing he could and his fingers found a leather strap that trailed from the ogre's chest armour. Ben's arm jerked tight and he heard the ogre growl in irritation.

"SQUASH LITTLE BUG," the ogre roared. A hand hit Ben with the force of a horse's kick. Fingers as long as Ben's legs wrapped around him, pinning his arms to his sides and crushing any hope of escape. He squirmed in the monster's grip, and saw himself reflected in its telescope-lens of an eye.

"So," said Scumbo, doing his best to smile. "You going to tie him up now or...?"

A tingling snaked along Ben's fingers. The metal of the gauntlet vibrated in his hand, but the ogre's fingers were like bands of steel, and no matter how he twisted and turned, he couldn't get his arm free.

THE SWIVEL-Eyed OGRE-Thing

Ben looked up as the ogre began to raise him higher. He was several metres off the ground now, close enough to the ogre's head to see the bristly hair in his piggy nostrils and the dark pupil of his one real eye.

The monster's breath swirled around him in clouds of stink and he realised its mouth was opening, the rusted cogs creaking as the bottom jaw swung wide.

"It's going to eat him!" Paradise realised. She shoved Wesley forwards. "Do something!"

"L-like what?"

Ben's head was within chomping distance of the ogre's mouth now. The monster's dark red tongue darted hungrily across its lips.

"Anything! But preferably not custard!"

Wesley gave a grim nod. He stepped nervously in front of the ogre. "Um, excuse me," he squeaked. "Down here."

"Now you're for it," said Scumbo. "This one's a wizard. He's going to stitch you right up, mate. Just you wait and see!"

THE SWIVEL-Eyed OGRE-Thing

The ogre paused with his mouth still open. His one good eye swivelled down until it found Wesley. "MORE BUGS," he boomed.

"Aha, well does a bug have one of these?" Wesley said. He shoved a hand up inside his sleeve and immediately whipped out a small bunch of daffodils. "No, wait, not that," he muttered, blushing slightly. He shoved the flowers back up his sleeve and fished around again. "One of these," he said, and this time he yanked out a slightly startled-looking red squirrel.

Paradise shook her head. "We're all doomed."

For a long time, Wesley just stared at the squirrel, and the squirrel stared back. Eventually, Wesley quietly cleared his throat and looked back up to the ogre. "Let's just

109

pretend this is a wand," he said weakly.

"Out of the way," said Paradise. She barged Wesley aside and grabbed the squirrel. Before the ogre knew what was happening she shoved the animal down the back of his boot. Almost immediately, the monster began to squirm and shake.

"TICKLES!" he roared. "MAKE TICKLE STOP!"

Releasing his grip on Ben, the ogre shoved a finger down inside his boot. Ben fell, down past the ogre's waist, down past Paradise, then down through the hole in the bridge. He hit the shallow water with more clatter than splash, and groaned as all the air was knocked from his lungs.

The ogre let out a sharp hiss and pulled his

finger free. The squirrel hung off the end of it by its teeth. The ogre tried squashing it between finger and thumb, but the squirrel released its grip and dropped to safety. It bounded towards Wesley, scampered up his robe, then shot back up the sleeve once more.

"Ben's hurt," said Paradise. "I'll help him. You keep this thing busy."

She raced down the bridge and vanished beneath it, leaving Wesley to face the ogre alone. It towered over him, four whole metres of muscle and machine.

"R-remember your training," Wesley whispered to himself. He raised his hands. His fingers began to dance in the air. "N-now then, Mr Ogre-thing," Wesley croaked, "you've got no one to blame for this but yourself."

And with that, Wesley made magic.

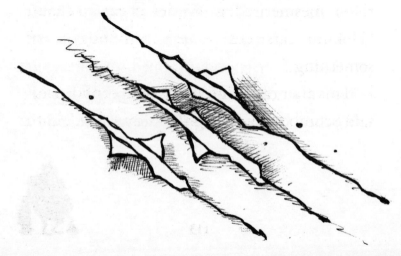

Chapter Eight

Sparks spun like tiny fireworks from the ends of Wesley's fingertips. The ogre watched them, mesmerised, as Wesley began to chant. "Hokum carsiccus ... er ... jimnus ... or something."

"This ain't really filling me with confidence," said Scumbo, but the ogre was transfixed, both glass and real eye focused on Wesley's sparkly fingers.

Wesley raised his hands higher as he brought the spell to a shaky conclusion. "Millinarus ... or millinarum, maybe? Poppakus ashtoomb!"

There was a bright flash and a bang and a puff of wispy white smoke. The sparks vanished and their hold over the ogre was broken. It blinked, as if awakening from a deep sleep.

"WHERE LIGHTS GO?"

Wesley stepped back. He had been hoping to turn the ogre into a duck. He had been *trying* to turn the ogre into a duck. And yet...

"I ... I don't understand," he whimpered. "It's still the same. Nothing happened!"

"Here," said Scumbo. "Where'd this hat come from?"

THE SWIVEL-EYED OGRE-THING

The troll was now wearing what looked like a jester's cap, complete with bells swinging from the three pointed corners. It was a little on the large side, and had slipped down so it half-covered his yellow eyes.

Wesley sighed. First custard, and now a jingly hat. He really was the worst wizard ever. "No idea," he lied. "Nothing to do with me."

The ogre's robotic leg hissed and clanked as it took a step in Wesley's direction. Wesley raised his hands again, but they were shaking too much for him to try any more magic. Instead, he held them up either side of his head in a gesture of surrender, and hoped the ogre might go easy on him.

"Step aside, Wes."

Ben marched back on to the bridge. His clothes were wet and blood trickled from a scrape that ran all the way down one of his bare legs. He gazed up at the ogre and flexed his fingers inside the gauntlet. That tickle of energy tingled along his arm, and there was

THE SWIVEL-EYED OGRE-Thing

that feeling again, like there was nothing he could not do.

"Put down the troll, and tell us what you've done with the others," Ben said. "And I promise not to hurt you."

The ogre cocked its head quizzically to one side, then it hurled its head back and let out a deep, rumbling laugh that rolled all the way to Mount Nochance before bouncing back again. Ben didn't flinch. He just kept staring up at the monster, his fingers flexing. In, out, in, out.

"So," he asked, when the ogre's laughter had died away. "What's your answer?"

"ANSWER IS NO, BUG!" the monster replied, and he brought his free hand smashing down.

Ben skipped back, then as the ogre's fist smashed through the wood of the bridge he shot forwards, using the brute's bulging muscles like steps. The power of the glove surged through not just his arm, but through the rest of him, too. It was the most magical item his Uncle Tavish had ever encountered, and Ben could feel that magic flowing through him now, every last drop of it.

He bounded up the ogre's bicep and swung with the gauntlet hand. There was a spark of metal on metal as his fist clanged against the

THE SWIVEL-Eyed OGRE-Thing

ogre's mechanical jaw. The monster's head snapped sharply back. Before its face could even register surprise Ben hit it again, across the leathery skin of its cheek this time. The blow twisted the ogre around, throwing Ben off balance. He tumbled backwards, but was already preparing himself for another attack on—

WHUMPF!

The ogre had spun in a complete circle. It swatted Ben out of the air, sending him skidding across the slippery wood of the bridge. Before he could clamber back to his feet the monster's finger and thumb clamped around the gauntlet. With the slightest of tugs it was pulled free, and all the energy Ben had felt buzzing through him fizzled away into nothing.

"Give that back!" Ben cried. "That's mine."

The ogre held the glove up to the lens in his eye socket. The outer ring of the lens spun as he brought the gauntlet into focus.

"NOT YOURS NOW," the ogre said. "MASTER'S NOW. THIS WHAT MASTER LOOKING FOR."

"Master? Is that your name?" asked Paradise.

The ogre grunted. "I IS NOT MASTER. MASTER IS MASTER. I IS DADSBUTT!"

Despite everything, Scumbo let out a snort of laughter. It made his new hat jingle merrily. "Dadsbutt. That's unfortunate."

"SHUT UP, TROLL!"

"Shutting up now," Scumbo squeaked.

"YOU IS COMING WITH ME!"

THE SWIVEL-Eyed OGRe-Thing

"No!" yelped Ben. "Let him go!"

Dadsbutt ignored him. Liquid burbled through the pipework in the ogre's mechanical leg as he squatted down low. Then, with a sudden kick, he leapt into the air and bounded off into the darkness.

Several seconds later, somewhere far away, they heard the muffled thud of him landing. They heard him land once more after that, further away still. And then they heard nothing but the babbling of the stream below.

"Well," breathed Wesley. "I think that went really rather well."

"Well?" said Paradise. "You thought that went well?"

"We're still alive, aren't we?" said Wesley. "And now we have information."

"What, that you're rubbish at magic? We already knew that."

"Dadsbutt," said Wesley. He rummaged up his sleeve, then pulled out his copy of Who's Who, What's What and Why They Do Such Horrible Things to One Another by Lunt Bingwood. He sat on the edge of the bridge and opened the cover. "I'm pretty sure he's in here somewhere."

THE SWIVEL-EYED OGRE-THING

As Wesley flicked through the pages, Ben looked down at his now bare right hand. "My glove," he said. "He took my glove."

"If it's any consolation, I doubt it'll fit him," Paradise said.

Wesley stood up sharply. "Aha! Yes, here he is. Dadsbutt the Ogre."

He turned the book around so the others could see the hand-drawn illustration of the monster they'd just fought. It had the same bone armour, the same mechanical leg.

The version in the book had two eyes, though, and nowhere near as many scars as the one in real life had.

"Looks a bit different," Paradise pointed out.

"Yes, well Lunt Bingwood did write the book over ten years ago," Wesley said. "Ogres don't age well."

"What does it say?" Ben asked.

Wesley angled the book so he could make out the scratchy writing in the torchlight, then began to read.

"As is traditional for ogres, the then baby Dadsbutt was named after the first thing he saw in the moments following his birth. Even by ogre standards, where names such as 'Table', 'Somerocks', and 'Mumsfeet' are not uncommon, 'Dadsbutt' was a particularly

THE SWIVEL-EYED OGRE-Thing

unfortunate title to be saddled with."

"I thought it quite suited him, actually," said Paradise.

"As a result," continued Wesley, "Dadsbutt grew up to be an angry young ogreling, quickly learning to rely on his brute strength and explosive temper to put an end to any childhood name-calling before it could even begin.

"In the years since then, Dadsbutt has developed a reputation as a near-unstoppable warrior. Despite sustaining numerous injuries in battle – including the loss of his leg and a good few too many blows to the head – the ogre continues to make his uniquely violent range of services available to the highest bidder."

"Master," Ben realised. "That's what he

meant when he said it was Master's glove now."

"He must be bringing it to whoever's paying him," Paradise said.

"And I bet that's where the trolls are, too," said Ben.

Paradise gestured to the book. "Does he have any weaknesses?"

Wesley scanned the page. "Yes!" he said. "A shocking disregard for the welfare of others."

"I think we figured that one out by ourselves."

"Anything else?" asked Ben. "Anything we can use against him?"

Wesley flipped to the next page, then flipped back. "No. Nothing. Sorry."

Ben smiled grimly. "Oh well. It was worth a try." He turned to Paradise. "Can you find them?"

THE SWIVEL-EYed OGRE-Thing

She nodded. "I think so, yes."

"Then get to it," said Ben. "We're going after them."

"Oh goody," said Wesley, trying his best to sound positive, but failing completely. "And then what?"

Ben rolled up the sleeves of his tunic and squared his shoulders. "And then," he said, "I'm going to get my glove back."

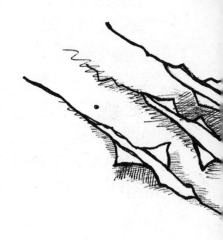

Chapter Nine

Ben and the others stood in the ruins of a village, gazing around at the rubble of houses and shops, and the burnt-out shell of an old wooden tavern. A stone well stood in the centre of the wreckage. It was the only thing that hadn't been completely and utterly destroyed.

"Dadsbutt must've done this," Wesley said,

THE SWIVEL-EYED OGRE-Thing

but Ben and Paradise both shook their heads.

"It was the Shark-Headed Bear-Thing," Paradise said.

Wesley jumped back in fright. "What, again?"

"No, last time," Ben said. "This is Paradise's village. This is what was left of Loosh after the Bear-Thing smashed the place up."

He looked around at the devastation. "I thought it was being rebuilt. The Mayor had all those building supplies sent over."

"It *is* being rebuilt," said Paradise, defensively. Ever since the Mayor had found her wandering the woods as a baby he had taken care of her. She trusted him with her life, and if he said he was rebuilding Loosh then he was. Admittedly, he seemed to be doing it much more slowly than she would have expected, but still. "These things take time, you know?"

"So ... why are we here, exactly?" Wesley asked. "I mean, not that I'm complaining, but I don't see any massive robo-ogres round here."

"He's close," Paradise said. She turned and scanned the trees to the east of the village. The dense forest stretched up the first few hundred metres of Mount Nochance, before the terrain became too steep and the trees decided that enough was enough, thank you very much,

THE SWIVEL-Eyed OGRE-Thing

and that they were all perfectly happy down on the flat bit anyway.

"Up there," Paradise said. "Dadsbutt and Scumbo, they're both up there."

"Then what are we waiting around here for?" asked Ben.

"When we should be running as fast as we can in the opposite direction!" added Wesley. He smiled hopefully at them. "No? Oh well. Worth a try."

Ben started towards the trees, but Paradise caught his arm. "Let's be careful," she said. "They're not alone."

"The trolls are there?"

"I think so," said Paradise. "And ... someone else. I don't know who, but I can feel them up there."

"Dadsbutt's master," Ben guessed.

"Whoever it is, I think he's waiting for you, Ben. I think he knows we're coming."

Ben nodded. "Good. Then I hope he has my glove ready."

"I doubt they'll give it up without a fight," said Wesley.

"That suits me fine," said Ben, heading up

into the forest.

They found Dadsbutt's trail almost at once. A wide expanse of grass had been flattened, and dozens of branches lay broken and trampled on the forest floor. Several large trees had been pushed over, their thick trunks snapped in two, their roots ripped free of their soil beds. It was a path of destruction that led straight into the shadowy heart of the woods.

"So ... I'm guessing this way?" said Ben.

Paradise nodded. Wesley groaned. Then all three of them followed in Dadsbutt's footsteps.

133

They stayed quiet, stayed alert, and stayed close together. The whole forest seemed to be holding its breath and watching them. Not a bird tweeted, not a leaf rustled as they crept on quietly through the woods.

And then, all of a sudden, they spied something through a gap in the trees – a long and narrow wooden hut with no windows and a heavy-looking door. It stood in a clearing all on its own. Ten metres or so beyond it, the rocky face of Mount Nochance rose sharply towards the sky.

Ben and the others ducked down low and scanned the area. Nobody moving. Nobody there.

"I think it's safe," Ben said.

"I highly doubt that," whispered Wesley.

THE SWIVEL-EYED OGRE-Thing

"Is Scumbo in there?"

Paradise nodded. "Him ... and I think a few others."

"What about Dadsbutt?"

"No, not there. He's..." She stopped.

"He's where?" whimpered Wesley. "And just so we're clear – if you say 'standing right behind you' I will die."

"No," said Paradise, shaking her head. "It's like he's inside the mountain itself."

Ben shrugged. "Good enough for me. I'm going to go rescue Scumbo."

"Are you absolutely sure that's such a good idea?" Wesley asked. "He does eat people, remember?"

"He only mostly eats them," Ben corrected.

"That might actually be worse."

135

"I promised him," Ben said. "I promised him he'd be safe."

"Yes, well," Wesley stumbled. "Maybe ... he's forgotten. Anyway, I'm sure we're worrying about nothing. For all we know he's having the time of his life in there!"

From somewhere nearby there came a muffled scream of pain.

"Although he probably isn't," Wesley admitted. He sighed. "Fine. Let's go get it over with."

They kept low, scampering across the flattened grass until they reached the back of the hut. Ben listened for any sign that they had been spotted, then sidled around the building until he found the door.

"Locked," he said, trying the handle.

THE SWIVEL-EYED OGRE-Thing

"Oh well, we did our best," Wesley offered. He patted Ben on the shoulder. "Can't win them all, I suppose."

Stepping back, Ben brought his boot up and slammed it against the door. A jolt of pain shot along his leg and he went sprawling backwards on to the forest floor.

The door, on the other hand, didn't budge.

"Ouch," he muttered. He stood up and took aim again. He locked his sights on a spot right by the door handle. He practised his leg swing a couple of times. He took a deep breath.

Before he could kick, Paradise caught him by the belt of his tunic and pulled him around the corner. "What are you——?" he began, but Wesley's hand clamped over his mouth. With a tilt of his head, Wesley gestured in the direction of Mount Nochance. Ben nodded to say he understood, and Wesley pulled his hand away.

Quietly, Ben leaned over to the corner and peeked out. There, stretching as he emerged from a dark cave in the mountainside, was Dadsbutt. The moonlight reflected off his scarred bald head.

Ben ducked out of sight just as the ogre turned towards the shed. The ground began to

THE SWIVEL-Eyed OGRE-Thing

shake, louder and louder, as Dadsbutt stomped closer and closer.

The children pressed themselves tightly against the wooden wall. Dadsbutt loomed taller than the building, and for one horrible moment Ben thought the ogre would look down and spot them. Instead, Dadsbutt knelt down at the door. They heard him muttering to himself, then there was a jangling of keys followed by the clunk of a lock.

Ben risked a glance around the corner. Dadsbutt was close enough to touch. The ogre had pushed the door open and had a hand shoved through the doorway all the way up to the elbow. The tip of his tongue stuck out through his metal teeth as he felt around inside the shed. From the other side of the wall came

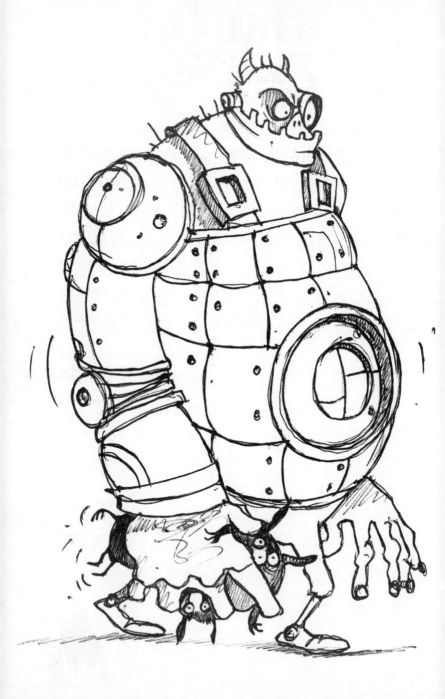

THE SWIVEL-EYED OGRE-THING

a series of panicky troll-like squeals.

With a grunt of triumph, Dadsbutt yanked his arm back out again. He held three trolls trapped between his limb-like fingers. Ben caught a fleeting glimpse of Scumbo's frightened-looking face poking out between the ogre's thumb and forefinger, then Dadsbutt locked the door, stood up, and thundered back in the direction of the cave.

"YOUR TURN LITTLE TROLLS," the monster said, and there was an even nastier edge to his voice than normal. "MASTER IS READY FOR YOU NOW!"

"What do we do?" asked Paradise.

"All in favour of running away?" said Wesley. He raised his hand into the air and glanced anxiously at the others.

"We need to get Ben's glove back."

"And save the trolls," added Ben.

Wesley thrust his hand higher. "Anyone?" he asked hopefully.

Ben and Paradise both shook their heads. Wesley sighed and lowered his arm. "N-no, thought not," he stammered, and he stuck close to Ben and Paradise as they hurried after Dadsbutt and in through the dark hole in the side of Mount Nochance.

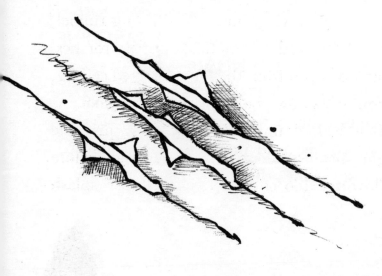

chapter Ten

Beyond the cave entrance was a long tunnel, lit on both sides by hundreds of fiery torches. Water dripped from the moss-covered ceiling, forming shallow pools on the uneven floor.

Ben waited until Dadsbutt was just the right distance along the passageway before following. Too close and one clumsy splash would be enough to give them away. Too far and the ogre might lose them in the next tunnel. They crept along in the middle of the path, where the torchlight was at its weakest.

Dadsbutt whistled tunelessly as he stomped along. The sound of the ogre's robotic leg reminded Ben of Uncle Tavish's arm. Ben knew the blacksmith would be worried sick by now, but there was no way he was letting Scumbo down, and no way he was going anywhere without his gauntlet.

It wasn't just that the glove was powerful, it was that it had once belonged to his parents, and that made it his most precious possession in all the world.

"What's that smell?" gasped Paradise, then she froze as her voice echoed all the way along

THE SWIVEL-EYED OGRE-THING

the tunnel, amplifying as it bounced from wall to wall.

The children ducked down in the shadows, but Dadsbutt kept walking, the thundering echo of his own footsteps drowning out all other sound.

Ben sniffed the air and immediately wished he hadn't. A truly foul stench snagged at the back of his throat and made his eyes water.

"Scumbo," Wesley wheezed. "Got to be."

"It's worse," said Paradise. "Although I didn't believe that was even possible."

Burying their noses in the crooks of their elbows, they pressed on, picking up their pace as they tried to close the gap between them and Dadsbutt. With a final few long strides, the ogre turned a corner at the end of the passageway and vanished out of sight. Ben broke into a run. He sprinted on as fast as he could, splashing through puddles and leaping lumps of rock. With every step the smell grew stronger, until the air was thick and choking with it.

Ben peered around the corner and the stench became almost too much to bear. The tunnel turned off into a wide cavern that was lit with

THE SWIVEL-EYED OGRE-Thing

an eerie green glow. Along the walls hung hundreds of glass jars, each one filled with a squirming bright green mass.

"Glowslugs," whispered Wesley, peeking into the cavern. "But I've never seen so many in one place."

Ben had barely noticed the glowslugs, though. His attention was instead focused on a metal construction that stood in the centre of the cave. It looked like a long narrow building, with round windows along each side. It was at least as long as Lump's main street, and stood three or more storeys high. It was impossible to say exactly how many floors it had, because the top of the building stretched out of sight through a hole in the cave ceiling.

The narrow end of the lowest floor was

THE SWIVEL-EYED OGRE-Thing

hinged at the bottom. It stood open, the wall forming a ramp up which Dadsbutt walked. Beyond the ogre, Ben could see four or five trolls. They sat on what looked like large metal buckets, straps and chains holding them in place. Brass pipes ran from the back of each bucket, before vanishing up through holes in the ceiling above them.

"What's happening to them?" Paradise asked. At first Ben didn't recognise her voice, then he realised she had shoved a small rock up each nostril in an attempt to block out the smell.

From inside the building there came a chorus of parps and phuts and impressively loud farts. They echoed around inside the buckets, then rattled noisily up the pipes.

"They're being harvested," Wesley realised. "They're being harvested for their gas!"

"So ... what?" frowned Ben. "Someone's collecting troll farts?"

"That's why they're using glowslugs to light the cave," Wesley realised. "One naked flame in here and the whole place would be wiped off the face of the map."

"Right, but why would anyone want to collect troll farts?" Ben asked.

Wesley shrugged. "To make the world's biggest stink bomb?"

Paradise spoke, but another round of thunderous parping drowned her out.

"As I was saying," she said, when the din had died away, "what do we do now?"

"You two free any trolls you can find. If you

THE SWIVEL-EYED OGRE-THING

see Dadsbutt, hide or run away."

Wesley gave a nod. "I am all about the hiding and the running away."

"What about you?" Paradise asked.

"I'm going after Scumbo," Ben told her. "Then I'm going to find my glove."

"You think it's in there somewhere?" asked Wesley.

"Fourth floor," said Paradise. "Left at the top of the stairs."

Ben flashed her a grateful smile. "Thanks," he said. "Any questions?"

Wesley raised a hand. "Could this all be just a terrible dream?"

"I don't think so," said Ben.

Wesley lowered his hand again. "That's a pity."

Ben gave his friend an encouraging clap on the shoulder. "Everything's going to be OK," he said. "You two hang back until I signal everything's clear."

"Good luck," Paradise told him. "Don't make me have to save your life again."

"Same to you," said Ben, then he turned and ran, crouched over, to the bottom of the ramp. The smell was definitely worse there, but he was getting used to it. His eyes had stopped watering, and his nostrils no longer felt like they were on fire. He stood at the bottom of the metal ramp and waited.

A moment later there came a deafening drum solo of bum eruptions. The noise covered the sounds of his footsteps as he hurried up the ramp and into the ground floor of the tower.

THE SWIVEL-EYED OGRE-Thing

The trolls grunted and muttered when they saw him, and at first he thought they had been gagged. Then he saw the mechanical arms lowering one by one from the ceiling. Each arm had a fork attached, and each fork had something small, green and terrible speared on its prongs.

"Sprouts." Ben grimaced as he watched a forkful being crammed into the mouth of a trapped and helpless troll. A metal band around the troll's head and jaw tightened, forcing it to chew and swallow. There were twelve trolls seated on buckets here, and every single one of them had a mouthful of sprouts.

A shudder travelled the length of Ben's spine as he realised he was witnessing pure evil in action. Sprouts! What kind of monster was he

dealing with?

"Don't worry, my friends are going to come and rescue you," Ben whispered. He beckoned over to Paradise and Wesley. There was a wide staircase at the back of the room. Ben was about to head for it when a thought struck him. "You won't eat them, will you?"

The trolls shook their heads as best they could.

"Right," said Ben. He made for the steps, then stopped again. "Like, any of them, I mean? No chewing arms off or any of that. Deal?"

As one, every troll in the room broke wind in perfect harmony. The sound that emerged was strangely haunting, like a solemn melody on an old church organ. It was also – in every

THE SWIVEL-EYED OGRE-Thing

sense of the word – breathtaking.

Ben blinked in the sudden heat of the waft. "I'll take that as a yes," he coughed, making for the stairs. They were ogre-sized and made of iron, and he had to scramble up them on hands and knees.

It was the same story on the floor above – twelve more trolls on twelve more buckets, with twelve more hydraulic arms pumping them full of greens.

"Rescue's coming," Ben promised, then he raced by them, their wind at his back, their furious chuffing egging him on as he made for another set of steps.

There were no trolls on the third floor, just a wide space packed with pot plants and flower petals. The smell was almost as overwhelming as the floors below, but in a very different way. By the time Ben was halfway to the stairs the whiff of troll gas was a fading memory, and he realised this whole floor was a smell cushion between the prisoners below and whatever lurked above.

Ben slowed when he reached the steps. He still hadn't come across Dadsbutt or Scumbo, and he suspected the building was about to run out of floors. They were in there somewhere,

and so was Ben's glove. If Ben could find
the gauntlet he might have a chance against
Dadsbutt and his mysterious master. Without
it, this would probably be the shortest rescue
attempt in history.

Slowly, step by step, Ben began to climb the
stairs.

The room above was much larger than those
below. It stretched out on all sides of the
staircase. The walls curved upwards from the
floor until they met a ceiling made of what
looked liked stretched pigskin. All around the
room, brass pipes fed up through the floor and
vanished into the mass of material overhead.
Banks of levers and switches and big brass
dials were mounted on a raised platform just
ahead of the stairs, and right beside them was

an old ship's steering wheel. There were three large open windows on the wall ahead of the wheel, and directly beyond them lay the rocky cavern wall.

Ben looked to his left, to where Paradise had said the gauntlet would be. As usual, she was right. The glove was there, just a few metres away from him. That was where the good news ended.

"Benjamin Blank. I have been expecting you," intoned a figure in a dark hooded robe. The man raised his right hand and clenched the fingers of Ben's gauntlet into a fist. "Let me guess. You're looking for this."

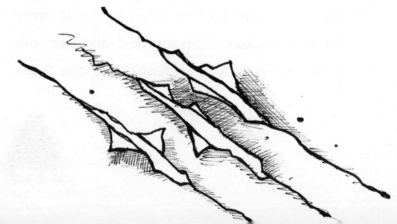

chapter Eleven

There was something disturbing about the hooded man's voice. It was only when he spoke again that Ben realised what it was. It sounded as if two people were speaking the same words at exactly the same time. One voice was deep and almost pleasant-sounding. The other was a whispery hiss that wormed inside Ben's head and made him think of nightmares long forgotten.

"Such a wonderful thing," said the figure, flexing his fingers. "Such power, such—"

Ben lunged. He threw himself forwards, making a desperate grab for the glove. The man in the hood made a gesture with the gauntlet and Ben jerked to a sudden stop. His arms and legs were pulled outwards until his body formed an X shape. He hung there, unable to move, floating just above the floor.

"As I was saying," continued the stranger. "Such wonderful little tricks."

The man came closer, his long grey robe swishing on the metal floor. His hood hung down over his face, so that Ben couldn't tell if he was even human.

"But that's all they are, really," he said, and that whisper echoed every word. "Tricks. I mean ... super strength. Portals! Such childish flights of fancy."

"Yeah, it's rubbish," said Ben. "Might as well give it back to me."

The man laughed at that. It was a sharp and hollow sound, and nothing like a real laugh at all. "Yes, quite," he said, then he turned away. "It's ironic, Benjamin. Dadsbutt thought I was looking for this glove, but the truth is quite the opposite. I knew precisely where this glove was. I have known for a very long time."

He looked back to Ben, and for a moment Ben thought he saw a glint of two red eyes in the shadow beneath the hood. "I was looking for the other one." He made that sound again that wasn't really a laugh. "You look surprised. Gloves come in pairs, Benjamin. I thought everyone knew that. Your parents certainly did."

THE SWIVEL-EYED OGRE-Thing

Ben jolted, as if a goat had butted him. "My ... parents?"

"Lovely couple. Such a terrible shame what happened to them," said the man in the robe, and this time only the whispering voice laughed. "But let's not talk about that."

"What do you know about my parents?" Ben demanded.

"I said, let's not talk about that," spat the man, in a voice that had become icy cold.

Ben's arms were starting to hurt. He tried to pull them down, but they were fixed in place. "Who are you?"

"My name is Antagonus. But soon you shall call me 'master'."

"I wouldn't count on that," said Ben.

"There are two gloves. There's the Alpha

Gauntlet – this one. And there's the Omega
Gauntlet, which I am on on the brink of
locating. When I do... When I have both
gauntlets in my possession, their power shall
be magnified a hundredfold. There will be
nothing I cannot do. You shall call me master
then, as shall the whole world."

A bell rang out from the console behind
him. Antagonus turned sharply, and studied
a number of dials and gauges. "Pressure,"
he muttered. "What's happening to the gas
pressure?"

"Oh yeah, I forgot to mention," said Ben.
"My friends are freeing all the trolls you
kidnapped. Hope that doesn't ruin your evil
plans or anything."

Antagonus whipped around, the gauntlet

THE SWIVEL-EYED OGRE-Thing

raised, his hand shaking with barely contained rage.

Destroy him.

The whisper spoke all on its own this time. Ben gasped as he felt his arms and legs being stretched further apart.

"No," said Antagonus. With his other hand he forced the gauntlet arm down by his side. "No, there is no need. I have all the gas I require, and even if not, I've always got the spares."

With a wave of his hand Antagonus turned Ben in the air. The hulking outline of Dadsbutt crouched at the far end of the room. Two trolls were strapped on more of the bucket contraptions, and the ogre was putting the finishing touches to restraining the third.

"Scumbo," called Ben, but the troll's mouth was already crammed with sprouts, and he could only trump noisily in response.

"So you see, Benjamin, your little plan has

THE SWIVEL-EYEd OGRE-Thing

failed," Antagonus said. "I have the Alpha Gauntlet, and the Omega shall soon be within my grasp. I sense it is close by, somewhere on this mountain."

He stepped closer, until Ben could hear his breath rasping in and out below the hood. "But don't worry. I am not going to kill you. Not yet. Not until I have made you watch everything your parents ever fought for turned to dust."

He paused to let his words sink in, but the moment was spoiled by an outburst of loud parping from the other end of the room.

"For now, though, I'd like you to do something for me," Antagonus said. He raised the gauntlet. "I'd like you to get off my airship."

Ben frowned. "Airship?" he said, then an invisible force hit him like a hammer-blow. He tumbled backward, spinning and rolling as he was hurled over the steering wheel and out through the wide-open window. His back slammed against the rocky stone wall, and then he was falling, sliding, tumbling down the gap between the mountain and the metal walls, the ground racing up to meet him.

He reached out, grasping for the trailing roots that stuck out here and there from the cavern wall. He flipped and rolled, the world a blur of rock and metal and sickly green light. His hands missed the roots, but his foot snagged on one and he jolted to a sudden painful stop just a metre or so from the floor.

With a groan, the metal wall lurched a few

centimetres towards him, and Ben felt sure it would squash him flat. Instead, the base of the towering construction raised off the floor. It moved slowly at first, but quickly picked up speed as it lifted up through the gap in the cavern roof.

"H-help!"

"What's happening?"

Ben hauled himself free of the roots and landed with a thump on his back. From the floor he caught a glimpse of Paradise and Wesley at the windows on the second storey. They leaned out, waving frantically at him.

"Look out!" Ben cried, pointing past them. They both looked up, then ducked inside just in time to avoid being smashed against the cave roof.

As the hulk of metal cleared the hole and
rose up into the open air, Ben was at last
able to see it all in one go. He could see the
two bottom floors where the trolls had been

trapped. He could see the storey above where flowers had covered every surface. Above that, jutting out on all sides was the much larger top floor he'd just been thrown out of, and above that...

Above that...

It was a balloon. The largest balloon Ben had ever seen. It dwarfed the rest of the airship – an enormous oval of pigskin that was swollen and fat with lighter-than-air troll gas.

Ben did the only thing he could think of. He ran.

Back along the tunnel he went, back through the forest and through the ruins of Loosh. It was a ten minute sprint back to his house from there. Ben did it in five.

Tavish was tinkering with some cogs and springs when Ben burst in through the door, puffing and panting and covered in mud. The blacksmith set down his tools and pushed his protective goggles up on to his forehead.

"There you are. What time do you call this?"

"No time to explain," Ben wheezed, too out

THE SWIVEL-Eyed OGRE-Thing

of breath to form sentences. "Bad guy. Airship. Dadsbutt."

"Dadsbutt?" gasped Tavish, leaping to his feet. "The ogre?"

Ben nodded. "You ... know him?"

Tavish hesitated. "What? Um, no. Never heard of him. Anyway ... airship? What do you mean, 'airship'?"

"Big balloon," said Ben, his breath gradually returning. "Bad guy has my glove. Says it's one of a pair. Says other one's up on Mount Nochance. He's going to get it."

"Wait, he has the gauntlet?" Tavish said. He sighed. "I knew I shouldn't have let you have it. You're too young to look after it properly."

"I have to go after them."

Tavish crossed his arms. "No. No way. It's far

too dangerous. I should have put my foot down at the start, no matter what the Soothsayer High Council might—"

"He has Wesley and Paradise!" Ben said.

That shut Tavish up. The blacksmith's eyes and mouth formed three little circles of shock. He tried to chew his fingernails, but picked the wrong hand and almost shattered his teeth on his metal fingers.

"We'll form a search party," he suggested.

"There's no time," cried Ben. "I got them into this. If anything happens to them it's my fault, so I am not going to let anything happen to them."

He stepped closer to the blacksmith and shot him a pleading look.

"Please, Uncle Tavish. You're the best

THE SWIVEL-EYED OGRE-Thing

inventor in the world. You must have something that can help me."

Tavish blushed modestly. He looked deep into Ben's eyes, and saw something there that was not to be argued with. A faint smile crept across the blacksmith's face. "Well, now that you mention it, there is a little something in my workshop I've been working on."

He gestured towards a door at the back of the house. "Shall we take a look?"

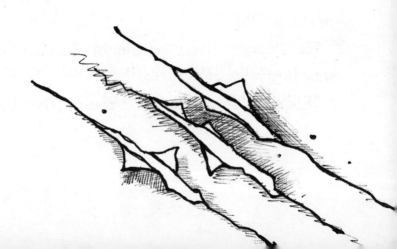

Chapter Twelve

Ben pedalled.

The wind whipped at his eyes. His legs ached. He still didn't quite believe this was actually working. But still he pedalled. It wasn't like he had a lot of choice.

The Pedal-Driven Feather-Based Vertical Transport Device, that's what Uncle Tavish

THE SWIVEL-EYED OGRE-Thing

had called it. He never had been very good at coming up with catchy names for things. Ben had immediately decided to call it the Flycycle instead.

His legs whirred round on the pedals, turning the chains that spun the cogs, which made the Flycycle's three-metre-long wings flap up and down above him. Far overhead, Ben could see the airship, already pushing up through the early-morning clouds as it rose up the side of Mount Nochance.

There were two things below him. One was the ground, and it was a frankly ridiculous distance away. The other was much, much closer and was either the best idea Ben had ever had, or the worst. Only time would tell for sure.

Gripping the handlebars, Ben stood up, his legs pumping harder on the pedals. The front wheel of the Flycycle angled upwards. The wings began to beat faster. Ben whooped with delight over the howling of the wind, as the gap between him and the airship rapidly began to close.

"We're done for," sobbed Wesley. He was sitting on the floor, his back against the wall, his head held between his knees.

"Try to relax," Paradise soothed. "Like we talked about. We have to stay calm."

"B-but—"

"I said we have to stay calm!" Paradise snapped. At the other end of the room, a dozen trolls jumped in fright.

The trolls were all huddled together, still recovering from their sprout ordeal. The door downstairs had slammed shut before any of them could escape, and the smell they were creating was making Paradise's head spin.

"Sorry, just … try to take deep breaths," she urged.

"If I take deep breaths in here my lungs might explode," Wesley pointed out. He stood up and began to pace nervously back and forth. "Oh this is hopeless. We're done for. Where's Ben anyway?"

"You know where he is. You saw him yourself, he..." Paradise stopped. A look of

THE SWIVEL-Eyed OGRE-Thing

surprise darted across her face as an impossible shape sped upwards past the window. "Oh," she said, racing over to look out.

"What? What is it?"

Paradise turned to Wesley, her eyes ablaze with excitement. "You are not going to believe what I just saw!"

Antagonus tapped a dial on a control panel to the right of the steering wheel, then shouted back over his shoulder. "More sprouts, Dadsbutt."

"N-not more!" begged Scumbo, trumping angrily into the bucket.

Antagonus spun on the spot. "Perhaps you'd prefer ... cabbage?" he said.

Scumbo's jaw dropped. "You wouldn't!"

Beneath his hood, a wicked grin crept across Antagonus's face. "Yes. I think it's time we hit them with the cabbage. Mr Dadsbutt, do the honours."

The ogre grunted. He unhooked a brown sack from the wall, rummaged inside, then bounced a cabbage off Scumbo's head.

"Ow!"

Antagonus sighed. "No, I didn't actually mean hit them with it, I meant feed it to them and..." He stopped. "What are you staring at, Dadsbutt? Why are you looking at me like that?"

Slowly, the ogre raised one hand. A scarred finger pointed past Antagonus and out into the sky beyond.

Antagonus turned. He squinted. There was

THE SWIVEL-EYED OGRE-THING

a pause before he said, "Is that a goat?"

With a *meh* that managed to sound both confused and furious at the same time, a goat came swinging in through the window on a length of rope.

Something that looked like a large mechanical bird flapped down into view. Pedalling steadily, Ben flashed the occupants of the airship a grin.

"Delivery for Antagonus," he said, then he twisted the handlebars and spun to the left as Antagonus fired an energy blast from the gauntlet. It scorched through the air, singeing one of the Flycycle's wings.

Ben felt the bike go heavy. It lurched sharply back to the right, sending his stomach up into his throat. The chain clanked, the cogs rattled,

and Antagonus took aim for a second shot.

"Oof!"

With a sudden lunge, the goat butted Antagonus in the groin. Crossing his legs, the villain sank to the floor, only for the goat to twist around and fire its back hooves into his ribs.

"D-Dadsbutt, help me!"

"DADSBUTT COMING, MASTER."

The ogre clanked and thudded across the floor, cracking his knuckles and snapping open his mechanical jaw.

"Bit quicker!" Antagonus wheezed, as the goat hoofed him in the stomach.

Outside, Ben's frantic pedalling was having little effect. Clumps of feathers drifted off on the breeze and the Flycycle bobbed unsteadily

in the air. There
was only one thing
for it. He had to kiss
the bike goodbye.

Gritting his teeth,
Ben hurled himself
towards the airship.
His fingers caught
the edge of the
window and his
body slapped against
the ship's metal
side. Glancing over
his shoulder he saw the Flycycle vanish
through the clouds as it plunged towards the
distant ground.

Kicking and heaving, Ben pulled himself

up into the airship. Antagonus was on the floor, trying to shield himself from the goat's furious kicks. Dadsbutt had almost reached him. There wasn't a second to lose.

Ben made a dive for the gauntlet, but Antagonus spotted him. A bolt of blue energy crackled from the tip of one of the gauntlet's fingers. Ducking, Ben felt a blast of heat whistle by above his head. The bright blue bolt bounced off a metal wall and began to ricochet around the room. It punched through a control panel, turning the switches to dribbles of melted metal.

With an ominous groan, the airship tilted to the left. Ben and Antagonus began to slide on the suddenly sloping floor. Ben grabbed for the glove and dug his fingers in under the

THE SWIVEL-EYED OGRE-Thing

cuff. He yanked sharply and felt it pull free of Antagonus's fingers, but then they clattered against the wall and he lost his grip.

Before Ben could move, Antagonus was on him, both hands on Ben's throat. Ben could hear his own heart thudding over the sounds of the howling wind outside, and of the goat headbutting the control panels to pieces.

"My airship!" the villain spat. "You've ruined my airship! Do you know how many pigs I had to skin just to make this thing? And you go and bring a wild goat on board!"

Struggling for breath, Ben managed a grin. "Yeah. And that's not all I brought."

Ribbit.

Antagonus's head tilted down. There, surrounded by straw in a large glass jar, was

an Explodi-Toad. Even through the hood, Ben heard Antagonus gulp.

"Picked it up before I came here," Ben explained. "You'd be amazed how fast that bike could go."

Antagonus was still staring at the toad. "You wouldn't."

"Oh, he so would," said Paradise. She and Wesley were clinging to the railing at the top of the stairs. "He's really reckless when it comes to stuff like that. I'd do what he says."

"One shake of that jar and this whole thing goes bang," Wesley added.

Dadsbutt stopped. Even his dim brain realised the danger the toad posed.

He wouldn't dare, hissed the whispering voice from beneath Antagonus's hood.

"He would," said Antagonus in the more human of his two voices. "He's got too much of his father in him."

Slowly, cautiously, the villain backed away. Ben sat up and thrust the jar towards him.

Antagonus gave a yelp and drew back against the wall.

"The glove," Ben said. "Give it back."

"It makes no difference," Antagonus spat. He slipped the gauntlet from his hand and tossed it across the room, well out of Ben's reach. "I'll get the Omega Gauntlet, then I'll come back for that one. It's not yours, you know. Not really. You're just keeping it safe for me until I want it back."

"Your ship's going down," Ben pointed out. "You'll never get the other glove."

"Come now, what sort of villain would I be if I didn't have a Plan B?" said Antagonus, and he made a dive for the window. There was a rope out there, tied around a metal hook. Antagonus hurriedly undid the knot and the

THE SWIVEL-EYED OGRE-Thing

rope began to rise.

Another balloon! Antagonus had another balloon!

"Goodbye, Benjamin," cried Antagonus, the wind whipping at his robe as the balloon pulled him out through the window. "See you again soon!"

Ben tried to make a dive for him, but a roar from Dadsbutt knocked him backwards off his feet.

"LEAVE MASTER ALONE!" the ogre snarled. He caught Ben by a foot and hurled him across the room. With a clank, Ben slammed against a wall, then tumbled down heavily on to the tilting floor. Raising his head, he saw the gauntlet. It was a few metres away, but slowly sliding closer.

Dadsbutt began to advance, but a tiny figure in a green robe blocked his path.

"No, you leave Ben alone!" Paradise warned him.

"Y-yes," agreed Wesley. "Leave him alone."

"OR WHAT?"

"Or you'll have h-her to answer to," said Wesley, quickly pointing to Paradise.

With a flick of his wrist, Dadsbutt sent both Paradise and Wesley sprawling. The ogre's one good eye fixed on Ben and he began to charge, faster and faster, his feet pounding like hammer blows on the metal floor.

The impact made the gauntlet slide faster. Ben grabbed for it and fumbled for the button on its back. Five strands of crackling purple energy streamed from the gauntlet's fingertips.

THE SWIVEL-EYED OGRE-Thing

Dadsbutt tried to stop running as a swirling portal opened in the air ahead of him. He tried, but he failed, and with a bellowing cry and a sound like a boot being pulled out of mud, he vanished into the hole.

With another press, Ben closed the portal before anything else could be pulled inside. He leapt up and bounded to the window, but Antagonus had already risen out of reach.

"He's getting away!" Ben cried.

Paradise thrust a jar into Ben's hands. "Not for long," she said.

Ben looked down at the jar. The bulging eyes of the Explodi-Toad seemed to wink back up at him. Ben leaned out of the window.

"Hey Antagonus!" he shouted.

Five or six metres above him, Antagonus looked down and spotted the jar. "You wouldn't," he said.

Paradise and Wesley both leaned out next to Ben.

"Oh," they said. "He really would."

THE SWIVEL-EYED OGRE-THING

And with that, Ben threw. They all watched the jar tumble as if in slow motion. End over end over end it went as it sailed up and up and—

BOOM!

The explosion came like the cry of an angry thunder god. The force of it rocked the airship, sending the balloon spinning into a spiralling dive.

"Did I get him?" Ben cried.

"You got us too!" Paradise cried. "You couldn't just wait until he'd floated off a bit, you had to throw it right away!"

"G-guys, please!" said Wesley. "Fight later. Now, try to stay alive."

The goat had wandered off now, and was quietly munching on some cabbage and sprouts. Wesley stumbled to what was left of the controls, trying desperately to make sense of the readings.

Ben shoved his hand into the Alpha Gauntlet and the aching in his muscles eased. He really needed to study it sometime, but Wesley was right – the first priority was not crashing and being blown to bits.

Paradise grabbed the wheel and struggled against it, fighting to level the ship off. There was a scraping of metal on rock as the lower floors brushed against the side of Mount Nochance, then they jerked free and the occupants of the airship found themselves spinning even faster, twisting in a hopeless spiral towards the ground.

"We're losing pressure!" Wesley yelped.

THE SWIVEL-EYED OGRE-Thing

"We can't slow down. We're going to crash!"

"If we crash we'll wipe half the kingdom off the map," Ben said.

"Then let's not crash," Paradise said. "Wesley, get downstairs, round up the trolls."

"And tell them what?"

"Tell them to fart," said Paradise. "Tell them to fart like they've never farted before!"

Chapter Thirteen

As it turned out, hurtling towards the ground in a highly explosive airship was pretty strong motivation when it came to farting. Fuelled by the sprouts the trolls parped and trumpeted for all they were worth, and slowly the pressure in the balloon began to build.

But still the airship dropped.

THE SWIVEL-EYED OGRE-Thing

"Two hundred metres," cried Ben, his eyes fixed on one of the few remaining instruments on the control panel. "One hundred and fifty metres. We're slowing, but we're not going to stop!"

"The cabbage!" shouted Scumbo from the back of the room. "Feed me the cabbage!"

"Wesley, go!" Paradise barked, just as the wizard reached the top of the stairs.

"What? How come I have to do it?"

"Just hurry up!"

Grumbling, Wesley hurried off to shove cabbage in Scumbo's revolting mouth, being careful not to accidentally stick an arm in.

"Seventy metres," Ben said.

"We're not going to make it!" cried Paradise.

"We're not done for yet," Ben told her. He

joined her at the wheel and they
heaved with all their might.
The nose of the balloon tilted
upwards a fraction, but they
were still spinning down, down,
down towards a particularly loud
and messy death.

"There," said Wesley. "I fed him
the cabbage, now can I please—"

A sound like a sonic boom
erupted from the far end of the
room. It blew Wesley off his feet
and roared up through the brass
pipework. The airship lurched.

"Twenty metres," Ben hissed. The tops of the trees were not far below them now. Any moment they would smash down into them, and everything would be over.

A second cabbagey rumble emerged from Scumbo, then a third. The ship jerked and jolted and bounced around in the air. Paradise gaped at the control panel, barely able to believe what she was seeing.

"Still at twenty metres," she gasped. "Pressure's holding. We did it! We stopped!"

"You're welcome," called Scumbo, as another parp lifted the airship several metres higher in the sky.

Ben sagged down and let out a sigh of relief. His glove tingled gently as he stepped back from the wheel. "Well then," he said with a

THE SWIVEL-Eyed OGRE-Thing

shaky smile. "Let's go home."

The whole of Lump and Loosh had gathered to watch as the airship bumped down just outside the village boundary. At first there had been panic as the door had opened and dozens of trolls had piled out – particularly from Mr Asquith the baker, who had already lost three limbs to a troll and had grown really quite attached to the fourth one.

But then a cheer had gone up as Paradise and Ben had appeared. Wesley raced past his friends, then spent a few minutes hugging the ground and crying. None of the villagers were entirely sure what they were cheering about, but the sheer spectacle of the thing made it difficult not to get a bit carried away.

Tavish smiled proudly at Ben as he and Paradise approached. "So the Pedal-Driven Feather-Based Vertical Transport Device worked, then?"

"It did," Ben said. "Although I prefer Flycycle."

Tavish tutted. "Flycycle? That's just silly." He looked around. "Where is it?"

Ben shifted uncomfortably. "Um yes. About that…"

"Where's the mayor?" asked Paradise, stretching on her tiptoes to see over the crowd.

Tavish shrugged. "Hmm? No idea," he said. "I haven't seen him since—"

"Here I am, my dear," said the mayor, pushing his way through the crowd.

Paradise threw her arms around him in a hug and just for a moment Ben thought he saw a flicker of pain on the mayor's face.

"Well, you've had quite an eventful night, it seems," he said, when Paradise had pulled away. "You must be exhausted."

"You can say that again," Paradise said.

"Yeah, I could sleep for a week," agreed Ben.

Tavish looked at his pocket watch. "It's a shame that school's starting in under an hour," he said. "You've been out all night."

Ben's eyes widened in horror. "What? But—"

"No way!" yelped Paradise.

"Mr Tavish is right," laughed the mayor. "Education is so important, don't you think? You run along to class. I'll look forward to

206

THE SWIVEL-EyED OGRE-Thing

hearing all about it at the end of the day."
He turned Ben's way just as a shadow passed
across his face. "*All* about it," he said, and Ben
felt the hairs on the back of his neck stand up.

"Come on," Ben told Paradise. "Let's get
Wesley and get this over with."

Keeping one eye on the mayor, Ben led
Paradise over to where the wizard still clung
to the grass. Taking an arm each they hoisted
him to his feet.

Behind them,
a hairy figure
in a jester's
hat stepped
out of the
airship and on
to the ramp.

Scumbo breathed deeply in through his
nostrils and raised his arms to the sky.

"Best game of Fart or Death ever!" he cried,
then he danced down the ramp to join the
other trolls. "Now then," he said, to no one in
particular. "I think I'll go see if I can fix up my
old bridge."

Ben and Paradise watched the troll trot off
on his merry way.

"Oh, Paradise, I forgot to say..." began Ben.

"What?"

"Saved your life!" he said, then he smiled,
heaved Wesley up over one shoulder, and they
all set off for school.

IF YOU HAVEN'T READ
BENJAMIN BLANK'S FIRST
ADVENTURE,

THE SHARK-Headed BEAR-Thing

THEN WHERE
HAVE YOU BEEN??

Turn the page for a sneaky peek at
what you're missing…

chapter One

Benjamin Blank was having a brilliant dream about kicking a giant up the bum when the world began to tremble. His eyes peeled open and he sat up on his horsehair mattress. The floorboards beneath him were rumbling and shaking.

"Earthquake," he whispered, then he yelled,

"Yes!" and punched the air. He'd never been in an earthquake before.

The rumbling stopped as suddenly as it had started, and he realised it probably wasn't an earthquake after all. There was silence for a moment, followed by a loud *boing*. Something shot into his bedroom through the wooden floor, then punched a hole in the thatched roof on its way back out again.

"Sorry!" called a voice from below. "My fault. Breakfast's ready!"

Ben clambered free of his knot of blankets, stretched, then slid down the spiral metal staircase that led into the room below.

A huge contraption filled one half of the circular room. Cogs clanked on the front of it. Steam hissed from little chimneys and water

THE SHARK-Headed BEAR-Thing

bubbled along narrow pipes. Somewhere, hidden in the inner workings, a chicken clucked impatiently. Ben hung back and eyed the machine warily.

"I built it while you were asleep. I call it the Automated Breakfast Producing Device," said Uncle Tavish, who'd never had a knack for catchy names. He stepped out from behind the thing and waved the mechanical arm he'd made for himself after he lost one of his own ones. It was twice as big as his other arm, and the movement almost made him fall over. "Watch this," he said, and he cranked a handle on the machine's side.

The cogs turned, the steam hissed and the chicken *quacked* in a very un-chicken like way. A small brown oval fired out from somewhere

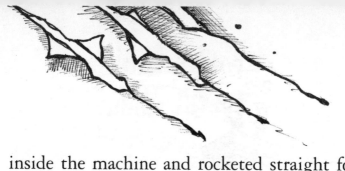

inside the machine and rocketed straight for Benjamin's head. Quick as a flash, he snatched it from the air just before it exploded against his face.

"An egg," Ben said, then he felt his fingers start to burn. He tossed the egg up and began to juggle with it. "Ouch, ouch. Hot, hot!"

"Well of course it's hot. Who'd want to eat cold eggs?" Tavish thought about this. "Unless at a picnic, perhaps. Or pickled eggs, obviously, mustn't forget them." His eyes lit up. "Ooh, an Automated Egg Pickling Device. I must write that down."

"Still hot!" yelped Ben, flicking the egg from one hand to the other.

"Ah yes, sorry," said Tavish. His mechanical arm *whirred* and the metal hand clamped shut around the egg. The shell splintered and a gooey blob of yellow yolk hit the floor with a *plop*. "Whoops," he said.